Double or Nothing

Double or Nothing
by MARC TALBERT

pictures by Toby Gowing

Dial Books for Young Readers

NEW YORK

Published by Dial Books for Young Readers
A Division of Penguin Books USA Inc.
375 Hudson Street ◆ New York, New York 10014

Text copyright © 1990 by Marc Talbert
Pictures copyright © 1990 by Toby Gowing
Designed by Judith M. Lanfredi
Printed in the U.S.A.
E
First Edition
10 9 8 7 6 5 4 3 2 1

Library of Congress Cataloging in Publication Data
Talbert, Marc, 1953–
Double or nothing
by Marc Talbert ; pictures by Toby Gowing
p.   cm.
Summary: Sam acquires from his beloved Uncle Frank
both a knowledge of magic tricks and
the wisdom to cope with the situation
when he loses his uncle.
ISBN 0-8037-0832-7
[1. Magic tricks—Fiction. 2. Uncles—Fiction.]
I. Gowing, Toby, ill. II. Title.
PZ7.T14145Do 1990 [Fic]—dc20 89-78315 CIP AC

Thanks to Justin and Caitlin Rhodes,
to Adam Fullerton, and to
Jorge the Magnificent

To Sheldon Fogelman,
for his magic
M. T.

Double or Nothing

*Sam was alone in his room now, sitting on the floor,
surrounded by boxes filled with magic tricks. He closed
his eyes to calm himself. It was like Christmas popping
up at the wrong time of the year—a drab Christmas
without wrapping paper or bows or carols or lights.
Large, sweating men had carried in box after box until they crowded the floor of his room. The smell of the
men still hung in the air.*

3

♠

Sam wasn't ready for Christmas. It was July, almost exactly between Christmases, and hot as blazes outside. He realized now that much of the fun of Christmas was thinking about it for a couple of months ahead of time—teasing himself about all the things he hoped to get but probably wouldn't and plotting what to get or make for his mother and father.

And for Uncle Frank.

When Sam was younger and thought about Christmas, he didn't think of Santa Claus. Instead, he'd thought of his Uncle Frank. He'd always been doubtful about the idea of Santa Claus. Each Santa Claus he'd ever seen—in shopping centers or on the street—had a moth-eaten beard that didn't move with his chin when he talked and usually wore a stained suit with the pointy ears of several lumpy pillows poking out every which way.

Santa Claus was a nice idea. But the story of Santa Claus, to Sam, was like a little white lie that got out of hand, getting bigger and bigger until finally people had expected him to believe that this fat old man slid down chimneys and flew through the air and spied on kids to find out if they were naughty or nice. Well, Sam remembered thinking, Santa Claus would need magic to do those things. Every chance he got, Sam

4

had looked for some kind of magic in Santa's eyes and hands, but each time he was disappointed.

Now, opening his eyes, Sam stared at the boxes stacked in front of him. His uncle hadn't looked anything like Santa Claus, but to Sam he was everything that people claimed Santa Claus was, especially when it came to magic. His uncle didn't go up or down chimneys, but he came through the front door and shouted "Merry Christmas!" in a voice that seemed to come more from his chest than from his mouth. And he brought boxes that held the most amazing presents—rocks that floated on water, stamps and coins from foreign countries, a piece of real sugar cane that filled his mouth with gentle sweetness, a miniature accordion that his uncle called a "suitcase piano."

And now Sam was surrounded by boxes of his uncle's magic tricks. He stared at them, trying not to think of why these boxes were here. It suddenly occurred to him that one of them might hold The Titanic, the fat, lazy rabbit that his uncle used to pull out of hats. He shook his head at the very idea—but bent over and listened a moment for half-hearted thumping. Just in case.

As he thought of the boxes and his uncle and The Titanic, it was as if two or three movies were showing at the same time in Sam's mind. He closed his eyes again and breathed deeply while the chatter in his head faded and the pictures turned to smoke.

The smoke began to clear and, in his mind, Sam saw himself as a three-year-old looking at a doorway that was open to the outside. It was his earliest memory. Sunlight glowed around the shadowy shape of a thin man with sagging shoulders, fuzzy through the screen door.

"You must be Sam," the shape said, its voice soft. "I'm your Uncle Frank. May I come in?"

Sam reached up for the handle, but the door pulled away from him before he could grab it, and the shape stepped through, his face and his body coming to life in the kitchen's light. The fall smell of burning leaves entered the kitchen with Uncle Frank.

Those eyes! When his uncle knelt in front of him, Sam found himself looking into bright blue eyes staring straight at him. He tried to beat back this staring with a stare of his own, but this worked as well as trying to beat back the light of one flashlight with the beam of another. The blue eyes searched his eyes, first one and then the other, making him squirm.

As he was going to look away, his uncle blinked. His uncle's eyes softened, the outside corners lifting up into

6

♣

many little smiles. Sam looked down as Uncle Frank reached out a hand—a large hand with long, delicate fingers. Sam reached out his own small hand and watched it disappear as his uncle's wrapped over and around it, close and tight as cellophane. They shook, Sam not getting it right, trying to move his hand up as his uncle brought it down.

When his uncle let go, Sam looked at his own hand with eyes that grew large and round. A half-dollar coin nestled where his uncle's palm had met his own.

Slowly this memory faded with the sound of his uncle's gentle laughter.

Sam sighed and opened his eyes. He'd kept that half-dollar all this time—almost five years. He stretched his legs so that they stuck out in front of him, reached into the pocket of his jeans, and pulled it out. He made a loose fist, his thumb cocked under the coin as it lay on top, and then flipped the disk into the air, higher than the tops of the boxes of magic.

"Heads," he whispered, catching the spinning coin and slapping it onto the back of his other hand. Whether he called "heads" or "tails," out of hundreds of times— perhaps thousands—Sam couldn't remember many times when he'd guessed wrong. It was magic—or at least Sam supposed it was.

♠

But since his uncle had died, Sam hadn't flipped his half-dollar. He was afraid that maybe the coin's magic was gone now—gone to wherever his uncle had gone. Slowly, he raised the hand covering the half-dollar and dipped his head closer. He peeked underneath, afraid of what he might see.

It was heads.

Sam sighed with relief, letting the coin slide bumping off his knuckles and into his other hand. He slipped the coin back into his pocket.

Looking up at the stacks around him, Sam was filled with a gurgling mixture of fear and sadness—and also of excitement.

I

Sam drew away from the mirror, his shoulders jerking back and forth as he fought for balance. He felt as clumsy as a dancing dog.

"Frigate!" he exploded, trying not to look at the cards in his hands. "Freight frigate!" he muttered so fiercely that his loose eyetooth wiggled.

The toilet lid he stood on had a broken hinge in the back, and one of its stubby rubber legs was missing. Sam shifted his feet farther apart so that the lid wouldn't wobble and clatter against the toilet bowl whenever he moved. The mirrored door of the medicine cabinet was open and facing him. Standing straighter, careful not to lose his balance, Sam stared at his reflection. Little beads of sweat clung to the tiny hairs of his upper lip and his eyebrows twitched in his frustration. A hank of straight black hair hung over his forehead and jiggled when his head moved.

He struggled with the slippery cards, trying to "see" them with his fingertips as well as if he were looking with his eyes. All his fingers "saw" was a disappointing jumbled mess, card corners poking out in all directions. Sam worked his fingers harder. Tomorrow, for the first time, he wanted to perform magic for an audience at Cathedral Park. And he wanted to be perfect.

As he continued to work on his cards, Sam wondered how long he'd been in the bathroom practicing. He didn't know exactly but it seemed like a long time. His fingers were stiff, telling him it was time to quit. For almost a month—since the boxes arrived—Sam had secretly practiced in the bathroom. Sometimes he felt silly keeping it a secret. His mother would have been thrilled. But he had a strong feeling that practicing magic was something between himself and his uncle, something they shared with each other and with nobody else right now. Sometimes Sam had the strangest feeling that, even though he saw only his own face in the mirror, his uncle was looking over

his shoulder, making certain that he was doing things correctly. To cover up his practicing, he flushed the toilet a couple of minutes before he quit.

He'd gotten really good at flushing the toilet while standing on one leg on top of the lid. Lifting his right leg, holding his breath as he struggled to keep his balance, he set his foot on top of the tank's lever. Carefully he cocked his foot and brought his heel down.

The swoosh of the water below was satisfying and the gurgle in the tank was relaxing. He slowly returned his foot to the lid. Less tense now, he studied himself in the mirror as he continued to work on the cards. He knew that Uncle Frank would have clucked his tongue and smiled at Sam's face. "The harder the trick, the easier you must make it look," he remembered his uncle once telling him.

Uncle Frank had made everything look easy. And fun. But right now Sam's face looked as if he were thumb-wrestling with a gorilla.

Sam lifted his frowning mouth into a smile— a stiff imitation of a smile that quickly faded. His loose tooth twitched as his tongue nervously flicked its smooth back. He pulled his eyebrows into an arch.

That's better, he thought. That's how I'll look when I do my magic at Cathedral Park. He closed his eyes for a moment, his fingers still working, and pictured himself standing on a park bench at Cathedral Park, in front of countless smiling faces. In his mind he saw his best friend, Charles, at his feet, with wide eyes, looking as if Sam were a movie star.

Sam wished his uncle could be there. Tomorrow was his uncle's birthday. He knew that he couldn't send his uncle a birthday package—the post office didn't deliver to wherever his uncle was. But Sam felt that his uncle, wherever he was, would be pleased to see that Sam was serious about becoming a professional magician—just as Uncle Frank had been.

Suddenly, Sam tilted dangerously to one side on the toilet lid. His eyes flew open and he clutched at the cards.

"Frigate!" he squeaked, quickly recovering his balance. He loved using that word because it sounded so much like swearing, even though he knew it was just the name for a kind of ship. He tasted a little blood as the tooth tore a bit more from his gums.

As he relaxed, he realized that the cards in his hands felt orderly. He glanced at them and saw a neat little brick. In his fear he'd squeezed them into place. I'll have to remember how to do that, he thought. He proudly stroked their smooth edges with his thumb, raised them to the level of his chin, backs up, and fanned them out like a bird's tail feathers. One more trick, he thought. One more trick and then I'm out of here.

"Pick a card. Any card," he chanted softly to his own face in the mirror, trying to make it sound like a command. Sometimes he had a hard time taking this pretending seriously.

He leaned closer to the mirror, daring the eyes he stared at to look away, feeling the deck of cards in his hand sitting properly, feeling balanced, one card ready to be plucked from the others. And then . . .

Pam! Pam!

Two sharp raps at the door startled him and he jerked up straight. Cards flew out of his hands, into the sink, and all over the floor. "Sam?" His mother's voice filled the bathroom. "You've been in there an awful long time. . . ."

The toilet lid slipped over the rim of the seat and his body was snapped forward. His tongue rammed into the loose tooth, popping it out of his mouth and into the sink. With a gasp, Sam grabbed the sink edge, panicking as the tooth scooted toward the open drain. He lunged for it, banging his head against the mirrored door of the medicine cabinet. The door crashed shut and bottles inside clanked against each other and then shuddered. And just as his hand closed over the tooth, his elbow knocked the toothpaste-stained glass from its place above the faucets and it fell to the floor, sharp sounds splintering the air.

"Sam! Are you all right?" Sam's mother opened the door just as he pushed himself up from the sink and stood once more on the toilet seat, his knees bent and wobbling.

Even though the medicine cabinet door was now facing away from him, he saw her in it. She appeared flat and far away, as if he were looking at a photograph of her viewed from the paper's edge. She stared at the floor, now littered with cards and broken glass, and then she looked up at him. "What in the world . . . " she began. He hunched, expecting her to grow angry at the mess in the bathroom. Instead, she laughed.

Surprised, Sam turned slowly around on the toilet lid, his feet feeling carefully for balance. The sharp, ragged edge of the tooth bit into his clenched hand.

"Oh, Sam," his mother sighed, still chuckling. "Just like Frank . . . spending *hours* in the bathroom practicing magic tricks in the mirror." A sadness crept into her face, replacing the laughter. "I told him once that he was going to wear out the mirror, that his reflection would be fixed onto the mirror forever so that when *I* looked into it all I would see would be *his* face."

She stooped to pick up a card that lay at her feet. "You were in here so long, I thought maybe you were sick. And then I heard the toilet flush and you didn't come out. Oh, well." She stood and held out the lone card to Sam with a flourish. "Pick a card. Any card." Her voice teased him gently.

Leaning over, he took the card from her. "Thanks." The first part of the word rushed out through the gap in his teeth, sounding hollow.

"Well, well." His mother squinted at his smile. "Looks like we'd better put in another call to the tooth fairy. What is that now, three down?"

"Five," he answered. "That makes five." He enjoyed the feel of air leaking from this new gap in his mouth as he said certain words.

"You're shedding teeth faster than a cat sheds hair."

Sam's grin was lopsided as he scrunched up one side of his mouth to poke the tip of his tongue through the new gap. Tasting blood, he explored the tender wound, feeling the pointy tip of the new tooth coming in. The gap was perfect for sticking a drinking straw through.

"You'd better stay put while I get a broom and clean up all the glass." And his mother disappeared from the doorway.

Sam turned around on the toilet, taking tiny ballerina steps on the balls of his feet. He pulled the mirrored door open until it faced him and then he grimaced into it, trying to see as many of his teeth as possible. He hooked his finger and pulled back one corner of his mouth and then the other, counting all of the baby teeth he had left. "Fifteen," he mumbled, tipping his head back to peer into the cave at the back of his mouth. He curled his tongue sideways so that he could better see the very last tooth. He'd gotten a quarter from the tooth fairy for each of his other teeth. If each baby tooth in his mouth was worth twenty-five cents, then . . .

His mother bustled in, humming as she often did when she was thinking. She leaned the dustpan against the open door and poked the broom behind the toilet, sweeping cards and pieces of glass toward her.

"Frank would be happy to know you're working on magic," she said, looking up at him and pausing for a moment in her sweeping. And then she smiled, trying to hide it by bending over to reach broken glass under the sink. "He certainly had better ways to shuffle cards and make glasses disappear, though."

When Sam thought back, the first birthday party he really remembered was his fifth. He had been told many times about the others—about how cute he was during his second birthday party when he tried to pat the cake and ended up with goo all the way to the elbow— about his fourth birthday, when he wrestled a birthday present away from his friend Charles, who suddenly wanted to keep it for himself.

♠

He was told all these things and when he thought back to these birthdays, he couldn't decide if he really remembered what had happened or if he only pictured what his parents had told him so many times.

But he remembered his fifth birthday as clearly as if it had just happened. For the first time, whenever he was asked how old he was, he didn't need to think about which fingers to hold up. He would hold up all the fingers of one hand. It was like finally being able to wave to the world.

Sam's memory of his fifth birthday party began as he'd shown his friends at the table how to eat birthday cake without using hands. First, he'd held his breath so he wouldn't breathe in the cake, and then closed his eyes because the cake was too close to see clearly as he leaned into it. Then, keeping his lips like a fish's mouth he'd sucked up big globs of cake. It had tasted delicious. He remembered looking up when he finished and seeing his mother walk in, carrying several presents stacked on top of each other.

He looked at her, licking cake and frosting from his mouth, his tongue sweeping off chunks of both. Peering at his mother through globs of white icing and coconut shavings that hung from his eyelashes, he saw her smile

♥

crumble as she realized what was happening. His skin crinkled with crumbs and frosting and coconut as he smiled at her—to let her know everything was all right.

He heard the kids around the table giggle. He must have looked very funny with bits of birthday cake stuck to the frosting that was smeared on his face.

"Well," his mother said, her eyebrows rising. He could tell that she didn't know whether to be stern or to ignore what had happened. When she squared her shoulders and took a deep breath, he knew she was going to be stern.

Sam tried unsuccessfully to lick a blob of frosting off the tip of his nose. He waited, hoping that his mother wouldn't be angry with him in front of his friends.

"Sam." His mother walked up behind him and took hold of the back of his chair. "I think you've shown your guests how not to eat their cake. You are five years old. Now that you're a big boy, you should act like a big boy." She pulled his chair from the table and helped him to his feet. "Go to the bathroom and clean yourself up."

He didn't argue, even though he heard something in her voice that told him she wasn't feeling as stern as she was acting. As he walked by Charles, he stuck out his tongue and made a face. Earlier Charles had

♦

told him that he could do anything he wanted on his birthday, and he guessed now that Charles was wrong and had known it all along.

When he got back to the party his face was cool and damp and clean, with just a little frosting still stuck to his hair in front. All his friends were finished with their cake and were staring at the stack of presents in the middle of the table.

Some of Sam's friends ripped the paper off their presents. Charles did. But Sam always took off the paper carefully, peeling the tape slowly. He liked to take his time—not so much time that people got bored, but enough time to make the other kids sit on the edges of their chairs, bouncing up and down, telling him to hurry.

Sam didn't remember any of the presents he got on his fifth birthday—except one. It came last, in a big box that his mother brought in all by itself, hugging it to her chest, her hands not quite meeting in front. He knew the moment he saw it that it was from Uncle Frank. It was so big that it wouldn't fit on the table, so his mother set it on the floor next to him. The others scrambled off their chairs and gathered around as he kneeled on his chair and began to unwrap the present.

Sam tried to be careful, but his fingers were shaking

♣

with excitement. Little bits of paper tore off with the tape. Finally, he couldn't stand it any longer and he tore at the paper, ripping it with his fingernails. Charles clapped his hands and laughed.

Underneath the paper was a large cardboard box with an envelope taped to the top. Sam opened the envelope and his mother read what was inside: "For Sam: Things are not always what they seem to be. Love, Uncle Frank."

It sounded nice—like something Uncle Frank would say—but like so many things his uncle said, it didn't make much sense to him. He tugged at the folded flaps that made up the top of the box and when they popped open he looked inside. Pulling out wads of crumpled newspaper, he reached deeper and deeper inside the box.

Finally, his hand hit something hard. He grabbed and pulled it out. It was a small box, long and flat. Puzzled, he pinched one end, opened the other, and peered inside.

Lying in the box was a folded scarf. Sam couldn't believe that this tiny scarf was the only thing in the big box. Handing the little, flat box to his mother, he leaned into the big box, throwing out more crumpled wads of paper and almost falling in head first.

He looked up only when his mother laughed and

23

♠

tapped his shoulder. "I don't think you'll find any more," she said. "Now watch carefully." He watched his mother hold the scarf up by one corner, letting it dangle in front of him and his friends. She picked up the dangling end with her other hand. "Now look carefully. What color is this scarf?" she asked.

"Red," said Charles before Sam could answer.

Sam's mother nodded and brought her hands together. "Abracadabra," she said, pulling her hands apart.

Sam's mouth dropped. Stretched between her hands was a yellow scarf.

"How . . . ?"

"I'll show you later." His mother quickly stuffed the scarf into her apron pocket. "We don't want to give away the magic secret, do we?"

Sam smiled every time he remembered this present from his uncle. It was a simple magic trick—but wonderful. He could do it even when he was five years old.

And whenever he did that trick, he remembered his uncle's words: "Things are not always what they seem to be."

2

Sam burst out of sleep. His eyes shot open and he sat up so quickly that he felt dizzy. He was charged with energy and jittery with excitement, his mind perking as fast as coffee on the stove.

His lips moved silently to the words and music in his head:

Happy birthday to you!
Happy birthday to you!
Happy birthday, dear Uncle-Phantasmagoric-
    the-Greatest-Magician-in-the-World-Fra-a-a-nk!
Happy birthday to you!

Uncle Frank's birthdays had always been as special to Sam as his own. For the past three years, his uncle had sent Sam presents on this day. "It's my birthday and I can do what I want," Uncle Frank explained the first time. They were wonderful, those gifts. But they came with a twist: They were completely taken apart and were in pieces. Last year Uncle Frank had sent him an old-fashioned pocket watch with an etched gold case and lots of thin metal wheels with teeth. Sam worked hours and hours putting it together. When he'd finally done what he could, he wound the watch carefully and watched as the hour hand spun quickly around the face of the watch. The minute hand didn't move at all.

"It sounds like my kind of watch," Uncle Frank said on the phone after he'd finished laughing. "I'll help you fix it when I visit next."

That visit never happened.

Sam shook this unhappy thought from his head. He was determined to make this a happy day, a day that Uncle Frank would be proud of.

And then he remembered his tooth.

Flipping onto his stomach, he reached under his pillow and patted the spot where he'd put his tooth the night before. His hand closed around the coolness of a coin. Hoping that his parents had forgotten to take the tooth—so that he could cash it in again—Sam grabbed the pillow with his other hand and flung it off the bed.

He didn't expect to see anything. But sitting where the pillow had been was another quarter. Sam's eyebrows rose in surprise. *Two* quarters for one tooth. Yesterday he'd figured that his mouth was worth fifteen times twenty-five cents or . . . three dollars and seventy-five cents. But now, at *fifty* cents a tooth his mouth was worth . . . seven and a half dollars! "Not enough to retire on," his uncle might have said. But Sam was impressed by the rising value of his baby teeth as he traced the tip of his tongue along their smooth backs.

He let his legs dangle as he looked at the floor, a long way down. When his uncle's boxes of magic had arrived, he and his father tried to make them fit under his bed, but there were too many of them. So Sam and his father made the space under his bed bigger by placing cinder blocks under each bed leg. Now the bed was almost as tall as Sam, and he needed to pull out a box to step on whenever he climbed up onto it.

Sam longed to open the boxes, but his mother had made him promise that he would open only one. She told him that he didn't have room enough to spread out all the things in all the boxes. She told him that one box was plenty of magic to work on for now.

He heard footsteps approaching and sat up straight just as his father's face appeared at the bedroom door.

"Good morning, sleepyhead," his father said, yawning but trying not to open his mouth. He came into the room. His voice was still rough with sleep and he smiled at Sam, raking his fingers through the thick hair that rose like trampled grass from the top of his head. "Tooth fairy visit last night?"

Sam hadn't told his parents yet that he didn't believe in the tooth fairy, that he couldn't remember a time when he had. He didn't want them to stop giving him quarters. Smiling up at his father, he nodded and picked up the quarters next to him. "She left me two quarters!"

"Two?" His father stepped closer and peered at the quarters. His pajamas were as saggy and tired as his sleep-softened face. "I thought the tooth fairy only left one quarter for each tooth. You didn't lose two teeth, did you?"

"No," Sam said, closing his hand tight in case his father decided to take one back.

"Hmmm." His father scratched the stubble on

his chin, making a noise like sandpaper rubbed lightly on wood. "We'll have to have a word with that tooth fairy. Seems a bit much to me. When *I* was a boy . . ." Catching himself, he closed his mouth and looked at Sam's face. "Sorry." He reached out and roughed up Sam's hair. "When I was a boy dinosaurs still walked where our house is right now and people never took baths. What do *I* know, anyway?" Yawning again, this time opening his mouth hippopotamus wide, Sam's father stumbled toward the door and then spun around. "I suppose the tooth fairy can afford fifty cents a tooth." He grinned, showing several dollars worth of his own teeth, and then padded out into the hall.

Sam sat for a moment, puzzled that his father was surprised that he got two quarters. "Oh, well," he sighed, dismissing the riddle. His father was always joking around and sometimes Sam didn't know when he was joking and when he was serious. Ignoring the box that was pulled out for him to step on, he slipped off his bed and landed on the floor with a thump. Peeling off his pajamas and then dressing quickly, he patted the outside of his pants pockets as he did every morning to make sure Uncle Frank's half-dollar was there.

Sam wished he could walk up to his parents and boldly say, "I'm going to Cathedral Park today. I'll be home for dinner." But he knew what would happen if he did. He felt guilty about tricking them, but he figured he had no choice. Normally he went to Charles's house each summer day during the week so that Charles's mother could look after him while his parents worked. Sam knew that neither his parents nor Charles's mother would let him go to Cathedral Park alone if he asked them. They were afraid to let him ride the bus into the heart of the city all by himself. They said it was dangerous. What they didn't know was that every once in a while he and Charles rode the buses anyway, just for kicks. Charles argued that going together wasn't the same as going alone. And Sam pointed out that their parents had never told them they couldn't go with each other. Even so, they knew that their parents would have been upset if they found out.

Sam walked into the kitchen trying to look the way he did every morning. He hoped he was getting it right.

"Good morning!" his mother said to him as she carried her empty coffee mug over to the sink. She was so cheerful that Sam didn't know if she realized it was Uncle Frank's birthday. "I hope you and Charles enjoy your last Friday before school."

Sam groaned. He'd forgotten. It was a cruel thing for his uncle to have a birthday right before school started. He was always impatient for this day to arrive, even as he tried to keep the first day of school from ever coming.

His father walked in, smelling of aftershave and adjusting the knot of his tie. "What a glorious day," he said to Sam, smiling. He said that every morning, even when it rained. Sam's father turned to his mother. "Ready?"

"I suppose." She let her shoulders sag. "I *hate* Fridays."

"And Mondays," his father said, "and . . ."

"Oh, stop!" Sam's mother planted a quick kiss on his lips to shut him up.

And then she turned to Sam. "Say hello to Mrs. Goodman for me." She bent over and kissed him on the forehead. "And be good."

Sam smiled up at her, hoping he looked innocent. He grew uncomfortable as his mother's eyes lingered on him, as if she was trying to read his thoughts and knew what he was planning to do today. And then, much to Sam's relief, his mother smiled, brushed the hair out of his eyes, and picked up her briefcase from where it sat next to the refrigerator.

"Good-bye!" he called as his parents stepped out the kitchen door to the car, arm in arm.

Sam listened to the car back down the driveway and then he rushed to the telephone. He punched at the numbers faster than he could remember them or say them out loud. But his fingers knew what they were doing—Charles's mom answered the phone.

"Hello?"

"Mrs. Goodman?" Sam gulped and locked his knees to keep them from shaking. "I won't be coming over today. I'm going into town with my parents to help my mother's secretary."

"That's nice," Mrs. Goodman said. Sam's knees relaxed with relief and he began to sink toward the floor. "I hope you have a good time. I'll see you tomorrow?"

"No," Sam said, stiffening his legs and standing up tall again. "Tomorrow's Saturday."

"Oh, that's right. The week's gone by so fast! And next week is school." Mrs. Goodman didn't sound very sad about that. "Well, I hope you pop over after school now and then to tell me how you're doing . . . and how Charles is doing." Sam couldn't help smiling. Charles was always getting into trouble at school and trying to keep his mother from finding out.

"O.K.," Sam said, knowing that he wouldn't tell her anything Charles didn't approve of first. "I will."

"Say hello to your mother for me," Mrs. Goodman said before she hung up.

Sam could hardly believe his luck. *It worked!* Even so, he hadn't enjoyed lying to Mrs. Goodman. She was always telling his mother what a wonderful child he was—how honest and polite and well behaved. He'd tried, but Sam just couldn't think of a way to go to Cathedral Park without tricking her or tricking his parents. Besides, Sam told himself, when you do magic you trick people—you make them believe something that isn't true. I'm going to be a magician today and I'm going to trick *lots* of people.

Even as he told himself this, he knew that tricking people with magic was different than lying to them. Somehow or other, and he wasn't quite sure why, Sam knew that magic was honest and lying was not. But he tried not to think of that. He didn't want to talk himself out of going to Cathedral Park.

"Oh, well," he muttered as he hurried back to his room. He dropped down to his knees in front of his bed. The boxes were arranged to look like a solid wall, but he pulled out the one that he used for a step and crawled into the secret hideaway under his bed. He followed the gap, feeling like a mole pushing darkness aside, until he reached a cubby hole in the far corner. He turned on the flashlight that hung from a string tied to a mattress button. The flashlight swayed and he followed the spot of light as it went back and forth and around, the light becoming long and thin as it approached the walls of his room and the wall of boxes in front of him.

Once more, for the millionth time, Sam longed to open his uncle's boxes to see what was inside. He breathed in their cardboard smell, a smell he slept with now, a smell that made him think of magic. He imagined all kinds of things in the boxes—large silver rings and top hats that collapsed, and cups and scarves and balls of different sizes, and boxes and wands that turned into flowers or snakes. He imagined all the kinds of things he'd seen his uncle use during his magic shows.

Sam had promised. But more important was the promise he'd made to himself. He'd promised himself that he wouldn't open other boxes until

he'd earned the right to open them—earned it by performing magic before an audience at Cathedral Park, just as his uncle had done when he was a boy. Reaching out a hand, Sam brushed his fingertips against one of the boxes. When he got back from Cathedral Park, he might let himself open another box. Maybe the one he was touching.

The spot of light from the flashlight passed several times over the magic tricks Sam had laid out the night before, ready for today—the two decks of cards, one regular and one called a stripped deck, and the four sponge balls that he had practiced and practiced with, and the silk scarf that changed colors.

The only thing that he didn't have ready for today was a magician's name. He'd been thinking of a name ever since he'd started practicing magic. But he hadn't been able to come up with one that fit, one that sounded right.

His uncle's professional name had been Phantasmagoric Frank. Sam had always liked that. It was mysterious, impressive, magical. It made Sam think of phantoms and ghosts—spirits that appeared when you least expected them and then disappeared in a flash.

Sam picked up the deck of regular cards and shuffled them as he tried, once again, to think of words that went with Sam, words that would make a good magician's name.

Silly Sam. He shook his head.
Sarcastic Sam. He shook his head harder.
Saintly Sam. He groaned.
Salty Sam. Simple Sam. Savage Sam.

He gave up.

He grabbed up his magic tricks and some money for the bus, and stuffed everything into the pockets of his uncle's old magician's jacket with its wide red and black stripes and big fake carnation in a wide, pointy lapel. Turning off the flashlight, he crawled out from under the bed, dragging his uncle's jacket behind him.

Putting on the jacket, Sam went into the bathroom to take one last look at himself in the mirror. Carefully, he climbed onto the toilet lid and opened the medicine cabinet door so that it faced him. The jacket helped. But Sam was disappointed that he didn't look more mysterious or clever—more like a magician. And then his uncle's words came back: "Things are not always what they seem to be."

Sam thought for a moment, his forehead wrinkling. The best thief is somebody who looks innocent. The funniest clown is the saddest-looking one. Maybe, Sam thought, a good magician is one who looks the most ordinary.

Sam's forehead relaxed and he pushed his reflection away as he closed the medicine cabinet door.

If the best magician looks the most ordinary, Sam thought, then I'm going to be great.

♣ ♠ ♥ ♦

When Sam was six he practiced the sponge-balls trick that his uncle had sent him until the balls were sticky with sweat. He wanted to surprise his uncle by being able to do the trick. But when Uncle Frank came for a visit, Sam still couldn't get it right, and he felt as if he'd let his uncle down.

"Watch carefully," his uncle said, taking from Sam the four balls, which were about three times the size of

♠

marbles. Uncle Frank looked up at him, one corner of his mouth twisted into a smile. "These are pretty sticky. What did you do, wash dishes with them?"

"No," Sam said impatiently, wanting to see how his uncle did the trick.

Uncle Frank gave Sam two of the sponge balls. Holding one with the thumb and fingers on his right hand, he said, "Timing is everything. Watch." He held out his left hand, palm up and empty. He brought the sponge ball to it and, as he wrapped his hand around the ball, he pulled his right hand away, looking like a cocked gun with his thumb up, his forefinger pointing.

"Tap my closed hand," Uncle Frank said, "and give me some of your magic by saying a magic word."

Sam reached out his hand and tapped his uncle's. "Abracadabra."

Uncle Frank smiled at him. And when he opened his hand, the sponge wasn't there.

Sam threw up his hands in frustration. "I try and I try and I still can't do it right." He stared at his uncle's empty left hand. "Frigate!"

His uncle laughed. "Nice word," he said. And then his face became serious. "Magic is harder than it looks, isn't it?" He opened his right hand and showed Sam where the ball had been hiding.

♥

"Yes, it is." Sam frowned. "When I try to do magic, I don't feel magical at all." He looked at his uncle. "Do you? I mean, when you do a magic trick, do you feel *the magic happening?*"

"That's a tough question." Now it was Uncle Frank's turn to frown. "Most of the time, I'd have to say no. No, I don't feel the magic happen. I'm too busy doing the tricks."

"Well then, where does the magic come from?" Sam leaned back in his chair and crossed his arms over his chest. He knew his chin was sticking out, but he didn't care. "Is there magic or is it make-believe?"

Uncle Frank stared, his blue eyes locked onto Sam's eyes, making it impossible for Sam to look away. "Do you believe that there is such a thing as magic?" Uncle Frank finally asked.

Sam thought for a moment, surprised by the question. When he was little, he'd believed in magical things—things like cartoons and talking puppets on television. He didn't know when he stopped believing that Big Bird was a real, live, talking bird or that Mickey Mouse lived with Snow White and the Seven Dwarfs in Disneyland.

Sam shook his head.

"You don't?" His uncle's eyebrows jumped in sur-

◆

*prise. "Well, now. I think you're wrong. I believe in
magic. Maybe not the kind of magic I believed in when
I was three or four years old. But an even better kind
of magic . . . real magic, not make-believe magic."*

*Sam tipped his head to one side and narrowed his
eyes as he stared at his uncle. He didn't know exactly
what his uncle was talking about. "If there's magic,
then why don't I feel it when I do magic?"*

*"Because," Uncle Frank replied, "I don't think the
magic comes from the magician. I think magic comes
from the people who are watching."*

*Sam hugged his chest harder. "You mean the magic
doesn't come from you? It comes from me?"*

*Uncle Frank nodded. "How can I explain?" he asked,
looking up at the ceiling. He pressed the tips of his
fingers together.*

*"Ah . . ." He smiled and looked back at Sam. "Magic
is like reading a book," he said, leaning forward, his
eyes sparkling. "You know that a writer chooses words
and puts them on paper. And you know that a writer
works hard to make the words beautiful and easy to
read and to understand." He studied Sam. "So far, so
good?"*

Sam nodded.

"Now, some people . . . most people . . . would say

that a writer, a good writer, performs magic . . . magic with words." He smiled and shook his head. "But that's not what I think. I think that the magic in books doesn't come from the writer. The magic in books comes from the reader."

Sam puzzled over this for a moment. For a second he thought he knew what his uncle was trying to say. But the next second he wasn't so sure.

"You see," Uncle Frank continued, "when you read a book, you *make* the words come alive in your head. You *give* the characters their faces and their voices. A good writer makes it easier for you to make the characters come alive, but the magic comes from you, *not* from the writer."

Sam thought about this for a moment. It was making sense. "You *do* the tricks . . . and I *do* the magic?" he asked. He liked that idea, even though he didn't know if he believed it any more than he believed in Santa Claus.

"That's right." His uncle spoke faster now that he was excited. "Sometimes I do tricks for people who don't have a single magical bone in their bodies. I can be clever and fancy and they don't see magic at all. All they see are clever and fancy tricks. Those are the kinds of people who look at beautiful paintings and all they

♠

think about is how much money they cost. Those are the people who see big trees and all they think about is how many leaves they'll have to rake in the fall. Does that make sense?"

Sam didn't know if it made sense or not, but he nodded and watched his uncle's smile grow larger.

"I think that the people who see magic instead of tricks—beauty instead of money or dead leaves—are the lucky ones."

"You mean you never feel the magic?" Sam asked, still a little confused.

"Oh, sometimes I do," his uncle replied. "And when I do it's wonderful. Sometimes I know a trick so well that it practically performs itself and I sit back like the audience and I feel the magic . . . from them to me and back again."

His uncle sat back in his chair and his eyes grew wide. "And when that happens," he said, "the magic is . . . doubled."

Uncle Frank picked up the sponge balls. "Did you know that this is one of the first tricks I ever learned. There are lots of things you can do with these little critters. Now watch this. . . ."

Smiling, Sam sat back and tried to send magic toward his uncle.

3

As Sam walked out of the bathroom, he tried to puff out his chest enough to fill the jacket. He didn't even come close. The jacket was big and floppy, and he had to roll up the sleeves before he could use his hands. The shoulders sagged toward his elbows, giving him lumps on his upper arms where he wished he had big muscles instead. The bulging jacket pockets banged against the front of his thighs as he pushed open the outside kitchen door. Carefully locking the door and then putting the key under the mat, he hurried down the sidewalk toward the bus stop several blocks from his house.

The day was already hot. Birds were hunched

on tree branches, sitting alone rather than in chatty groups. The yappy dog next door stared from where it lay, not even bothering to growl as Sam forced his way through the thick, hot air.

Whenever a car drove by, he slouched his shoulders and pulled his head into the jacket turtle-style, hoping that he wouldn't be spotted by anyone who knew him. If he were seen by some nosy neighbors, they would surely tell Mrs. Goodman. And then it was only a matter of time—a very short time—before his parents would find out. Bad news traveled fast in his neighborhood. Bad news like the time when he was four and it was raining and he took off all his clothes and hid them under a tree so that they wouldn't get wet and yucky as he ran home from Charles's house. His mother had been waiting for him at the door with a big beach towel, holding up one corner to cover a smile.

Think invisible. Turning up the jacket's collar, he kept his eyes focused straight ahead, hoping that if he didn't see any people he knew, they wouldn't be able to see him either. "Invisible, invisible, invisible," he muttered aloud, sounding like a distant, chugging train.

"Hey, Sam!"

Sam jumped at the sound of Charles's voice. "Wait up!"

Sam pretended not to hear and walked faster. "Invisible, invisible, invisible." The train was getting closer and louder.

"What's your hurry? Hey! What's that *thing* you're wearing?"

The voice was right next to him, and he turned his head to squint beyond the pointy ears of the collar. Charles rode his bike alongside him, with a grin on his face that only a mother beaver could love.

"Hi," Charles puffed, his long hair soggy with sweat. "Where you going? I thought you were going to be with your mom and dad." The front of the bike wobbled from going so slow.

Rats, Sam thought. He tried to smile, even though that was the last thing he felt like doing. His thoughts were like a swarm of flies and one popped out of his mouth, buzzing. "I'm meeting them downtown. I had to clean my room this morning and they couldn't wait. I'm going to take the bus to Cathedral Park and meet them there."

"All by yourself? They're letting you go on the bus all by yourself?" The front wheel of Charles's

bike jerked sharply to the left. He hopped off before it tipped onto its side, and he ran, pushing it up the sidewalk alongside Sam.

Sam nodded, looking grim.

Charles's whole face pulled up into a smile. "Neat! Can I go too? Can I, huh? If I tell my mother, can I go? Huh? Huh?"

Frigate, Sam thought, a sinking feeling in his gut. But before he could say anything, Charles continued his pestering, using the same voice he used in a grocery store when he begged his mother for candy.

"Could I go with you? Otherwise I'll have to go with my mother to buy school clothes and get a haircut for the first day of school. A haircut! Cripes! I don't want to get a haircut. Everybody will make fun of me. I like my hair just the way it is."

As Charles talked, he jerked his bike back and forth, making the front tire bounce off the cement higher and higher, wider and wider. Sam moved away from him, hugging the edge of the sidewalk. "And she'll make me try on *hundreds* of pants and shirts and she'll want to be in the dressing room *with* me and she'll probably buy me new *underwear* because she'll think the ones I've got on are yucky. And new *socks* too that will make my *feet* itch. And

I'll have to walk around with *tags* hanging out all over the place and people will *stare* at me and tell her that they're a little *big* now but I'll grow *into* them. And . . ."

"Can you keep a secret?" Sam asked, not feeling terribly sorry for Charles. His mother was going to do the same thing to him in the morning.

Charles swallowed what he was going to say and nodded, leaning eagerly over the handlebars of his bike so that he could peer around the jacket collar and glimpse Sam's frowning face.

"After I visit Mom's office, Dad's going to take me to the art museum." Sam made his voice sound disgusted. He knew how much Charles disliked this place where people felt they had to whisper instead of talk as they walked around staring at portraits of people who'd been dead forever and naked people lying around with angels flying above them, in the clouds. Sam felt the same way. He knew that Charles was as spooked as he was, listening to whispers echoing all over the place and not knowing where the voices were coming from. Sometimes it seemed as if the voices were coming from the people in the paintings—the people who had been dead forever.

"I bet if you told your mom, she'd want you to go to the museum too."

"*That's* why you're all dressed up." Charles mounted his bike. "No thank you." He leaned back and jerked the front of his bike up and backward, making it rear like a horse. Charles shot ahead on the sidewalk and looped the bike around the mouth of a driveway, into the street, and then back toward Sam. "See you around," he called as he swooped by, standing so that he could pedal harder.

Sam's shoulders drooped in relief. Wow! That was close. He broke into a trot as the bus stop came into view.

Standing by the lamppost, he heard a rumble and turned to look, hoping to see the bus with its lighted forehead saying CATHEDRAL PARK. Instead, he saw a garbage truck barreling down the street, lopsided and streaked with garbage.

It passed, leaving behind a sour, oily smell. Disappointed, Sam looked toward downtown. The blunt tops of several tall buildings rose above a dirty yellow cloud. A car sputtered by, quickly followed by the purr of a sports car going into the city.

At last he heard the unmistakable rumble of a

bus approaching from behind and the wheeze of its brakes. He turned just as the door opened, stepped inside, and reached into the right pocket of his jeans for his bus fare. Reaching deeper and deeper, he fanned out his fingers. He didn't feel his money. He reached wider and deeper in the pocket and then jammed his left hand into his other pocket, just in case.

His pockets were empty. Frigate, he thought.

"Could you hurry it up, sonny?" the driver snapped.

Sam was embarrassed and didn't look up at the driver. And then he remembered putting his money in his jacket pockets, along with the magic tricks. Yanking his hands out of his jeans pockets, he plunged them into the pockets of his uncle's jacket. Instead of hitting the pocket bottoms, his hands slipped downward and forward, deeper and deeper, encountering pockets within pockets within pockets, until he was up to his elbows in pockets.

His eyes widened as his right hand felt a round disk somewhere in the depths of the jacket.

"Sonny, would you mind . . ."

"Here!" Sam exclaimed, drawing his right hand out of the pocket. He opened it and saw not one, but two quarters. Stepping up to the driver, he plunked one of them into the money box and walked halfway up the aisle, past the only two other people on the bus.

Sam was trembling as he scooted over to a window seat. He lost his balance and was thrown backward as the bus swung into its lane of traffic and trundled off down the street. Strange, strange, strange, he thought as he tried to get comfortable. To calm himself, he stared out the grimy window, but his mind wouldn't let go of what had just happened. First two quarters for one tooth and now two quarters appearing in pockets he didn't even know his uncle's jacket had.

He rolled the remaining quarter end over end in his hand until the bus began to shake too much. It lurched down the street and Sam watched people on the sidewalks. The closer he got to the center of town, the more people he saw—people plodding with packages or pushing carriages as if they contained thousand-pound babies, or just walking all by themselves with hunched shoulders and blank faces. They all looked as if they'd just been scolded. Parents pulled children after them and the children trotted and stumbled behind, bouncing and skipping each time their parents took a step.

Everybody looked drab. Sam polished the window with the heel of the hand that held the quarter, thinking that the murkiness might be caused by grime. But even through the clean circle he made, everybody looked the same as before.

Nobody looks happy. Sam was amazed by this thought. They look as if they don't have magic in their lives.

He remembered his uncle's shocked face when he'd asked him if there was such a thing as magic.

Where's the magic? The people on the streets made him feel empty and sad and he turned away from them.

He opened his hand and looked at the quarter, thinking that maybe he'd seen it before. One of the quarters under his pillow perhaps?

And then, with a start, Sam realized that when he was searching his pants pockets for the bus money, he hadn't felt the half-dollar coin he always kept there. Scrunching down in his seat, he frantically felt around inside his pockets, finally pulling them inside out.

He could have sworn the half-dollar was there when he patted his jeans that morning.

And now it was gone.

♣ ♠ ♥ ♦

Once when Sam was almost five, he was standing on a chair, leaning over the kitchen sink, eating a pickle that was about as big as an ice cream cone, when the phone began to ring. He let it ring a few times, licking and nibbling on the pickle the same way he ate ice cream, feeling pickle juice run over his chin, wondering who could be calling. Maybe it was Charles,

♠

asking him to come over to play. Maybe it was his father, saying he was going to be late from playing golf.

And then he thought that maybe it was his mother, who'd gone off to buy a few things for dinner, calling to make sure he was all right. His mother didn't often leave him alone in the house, and she might think something terrible had happened if he didn't answer the telephone.

As he listened, the telephone seemed to ring louder and louder, as if the person at the other end were getting angry—or scared. Sam jammed the pickle into the pocket of his shirt, wiped his hands off on his jeans, and jumped off the chair. He walked to the telephone, which hung on the wall, reached up, and jumped. He grabbed just as it rang and pulled it down to his ear.

"Hello?" he asked, hoping that his mother wasn't angry because he'd taken so long.

"Hello?" came an echo from the other end of the line.

"Hello?" Sam asked again, a little louder, hearing little crackling noises.

"Marjorie?"

Sam cleared his throat. "No." He didn't like people to mistake him for his mother.

"Who is this?" The voice seemed far away.

"This is Sam."

"Well, imagine that! This is your Uncle Frank. How are you?"

Uncle Frank! Sam stood straighter and pressed the telephone against his ear until the side of his head ached. "I'm O.K.," he said, trying to picture his uncle talking on the other end of the telephone.

"Good. Good. Hey, Sam? I can't talk long and I've got to speak with your mother. Is she there?"

"No," Sam said.

"Is your father there?"

"No." Sam wondered if he should remind Uncle Frank that his birthday was coming up.

"Then would you take a message for me?"

Sam thought about that for a moment, licking the tips of his fingers and tasting the wonderful sour saltiness of his pickle.

"Do you have a pencil?" his uncle asked.

"No." Sam wondered where his uncle was calling from.

"Would you please get one . . . quickly?" Sam could hear noises coming from behind his uncle, but he didn't know exactly what could be making them. Cars perhaps?

"Sure." Sam let go of the receiver and watched for

a moment as it bounced up and down and twirled on its curly cord, spinning on its head when it touched the floor. And then he trotted over to the corner of the kitchen counter where his mother made shopping notes. Trotting back with a long, yellow pencil, he picked up the dangling phone and held it to his ear.

"Hello?" he asked.

"Got the pencil?"

"Yeah."

"Good." Uncle Frank sounded pleased. "Do you have something to write on?"

Sam looked at the white kitchen wall in front of him. "Yeah," he said.

"Good. Would you write down this number and tell your mother to call me as soon as possible?"

Sam thought for a moment.

"Sam? Are you there, Sam?"

Sam nodded, as if his uncle were watching. "I can't write," he said.

"I beg your pardon?"

"I can't write," Sam repeated. "I don't know how."

Sam listened for a moment to the crackling noise in the phone. And then his uncle laughed.

"Well, I guess I should have known. You'll be five next week, won't you?" Sam nodded, pleased that his

uncle remembered. "*Do you think you could remember the number if I tell you?*"

Sam didn't think so. But he didn't want to admit that to his uncle.

"*Sam?*"

"*Yeah?*"

"*I think you can remember it if you practice it and practice it and practice it . . . you know, say it over and over again. Here, let me give you the first three numbers.*"

Sam listened.

"*What are those numbers, Sam?*"

Sam thought for a moment. He felt pickle juice leaking out of his pocket and running down his chest. "*Four, one, three?*" he asked.

"*No,*" his uncle said. "*Let me try this. I really should get off the phone, but this is too much fun. Got your pencil?*"

Sam nodded.

"*Good,*" his uncle said, as if he'd seen him. "*Got something to write on?*"

"*Yeah.*" Sam put the pencil's pointed tip up to the kitchen wall.

"*Good boy!*" His uncle sounded pleased. "*Now, the first number is a* one, *so I want you to make a circle*

♠

with your pencil . . . just one circle, a small circle, all by itself.”

Sam made a circle on the wall in front of him. He tipped his head to one side and looked at it. It was a good circle. He liked it. “O.K.,” he said, pleased with himself.

“Good! Now the next number is a seven. *Can you count to seven, Sam?”*

What a silly question, Sam thought. “Sure. One-twothreefourfivesixseven,” he said quickly, all in one breath.

“Great! Now, right below that first circle, I want you to make a row of seven little circles, baby circles, big one after the other, as quickly as you can.”

Sam continued to draw circles on the kitchen wall, line after line of them as his uncle told him how many. Sam liked his circles. Some of them were small and round as buttons. Some of them were long and squished down. Some looked like funny balloons. The wall below the telephone was filled with circles, rows of circles, wonderful circles.

When the rows of circles reached almost to the floor, his uncle stopped. “That’s all, Sam. I’ve really got to get off the phone or I’ll never be able to pay my bill.

Be sure to tell your mother I called. And give her this telephone number . . . all of these numbers . . . just the way you wrote them down. O.K.?"

"O.K.," Sam said. He looked at the circles and thought some of them would look neat if they were turned into baseballs or golf balls or . . .

"And don't mess with them until you show your mother," Uncle Frank said, as if he could read Sam's mind. "O.K.?"

"O.K." Sam sighed.

"I'll talk with you later. O.K.?"

"O.K."

"Good-bye."

"Good-bye."

And then his uncle hung up. Sam jumped as high as he could several times before the telephone stayed on its hook.

He stuck the pencil into the right front pocket of his jeans as he walked to the sink. Climbing onto the chair, he pulled the pickle out of his shirt pocket. His shirt was soaked in front but the pickle looked all right.

He was taking his second big bite when his mother walked into the kitchen, carrying a grocery sack in each arm.

"Hello, Sam. Everything O.K. while I was gone?"

Sam's mouth was full, so he nodded. A drop of pickle juice flicked off from his chin and onto the floor.

His mother walked over to the counter and let go of the sacks. Shaking her arms loose, she walked over to Sam, smiling. "You sure take your pickle-eating seriously, don't you."

He nodded.

"Would you help me unpack?" Sam nodded again. "But first I need to make a phone call." She turned, took a step toward the telephone, and stopped. "What in the world happened to the wall?" She turned back to Sam.

Sam swallowed. "Uncle Frank called."

His mother's mouth moved up and down and out as she squinted at him. "What does that have to do with the kitchen wall?" She reached over, pulled the pencil out of the pocket of his jeans, and wagged it at him.

"That's his telephone number," Sam said. "He wants you to call him back. Now."

His mother stopped wagging the pencil and looked at the wall. "A telephone number. How . . ."

"Easy," Sam said, hopping off the chair and walking past his mother. He pointed at the circles with what was left of his pickle. "This is a one. See? It's just one

♣

circle. This is a seven *because it has seven circles. See?"*

His mother threw up her hands and laughed. "All right already," she said. "I should have known. But why did you write it on the wall?"

Sam tried to remember exactly what Uncle Frank had said. "Uncle Frank told me to."

"Hmmm." His mother looked at him doubtfully. "I guess there's only one way to find out." She walked to the telephone and dialed, looking at the wall and counting circles before she punched in each number. And then she waited while it rang at the other end.

"May I speak to Frank Ellis, please?" She was looking at Sam as she spoke and she continued to study him as she waited. "Frank? This is your sister calling. . . . Fine, fine. . . . Hey, Frank, I have a question for you. . . ."

Sam stuck the last big bite of pickle into his mouth and walked out the kitchen door chewing, thinking about the number on the wall. And as he walked into his backyard, he remembered each number he'd written down using circles.

It was a number he'd never forget.

4

The bus veered and then stopped at the main gate to Cathedral Park. Sam had been searching his inside-out pockets for holes, and, sure enough, he'd found one large enough for a half-dollar coin to slip through. Hurriedly, he stuffed the pockets back into his jeans and then crab-walked over the seat to the aisle.

"Frigate," he muttered as his jacket snagged the armrest when he stood. Yanking the jacket loose, he rushed toward the front of the bus. People were already climbing inside and he squeezed his way past their legs and through their shopping bags and purses and briefcases. Stumbling down the stairs, he pushed out of the door and onto the sidewalk.

The day had grown hotter and sweat trickled down his spine. Sam stood for a moment and frowned, feeling terrible about losing the half-dollar his uncle had given him, angrily fanning himself with the front flaps of his jacket. He looked at the arched brick gate to the park, making kissing noises as he sucked at the gap in his teeth.

He was certain that he'd had it this morning when he put on his jeans—it had felt cold on his thigh and then quickly warmed against his skin so that it seemed to melt into his leg. As always, he'd patted the pocket for its hardness. But it had surely slipped through the hole, along with the kind of fuzz that collects in pockets and belly buttons.

"Freight frigate," he muttered, air making angry, swooshing sounds through the gap in his teeth. He was so upset that he felt like crying. *"Freight frigate . . . floundering!"*

"Pardon," a woman puffed, brushing against him as she hurried past. He glared at her as she walked away. And then the bus behind him roared, making him jump. Stepping away from the exhaust, he grew angrier still. He wanted to roar back at the bus. He wanted a terrible sound to come billowing out of his mouth—a sound that people could see—a sound as black and smelly as the exhaust from the bus—a sound that people would have to breathe in as well as hear—a sound that would fill their lungs and make them cough and make tears come to their burning eyes.

And then right in front of him trotted a large yellow dog, with a sagging back and drooping belly, carrying a plastic bag of hot dog buns in its mouth as if the bag were a purse. Its tail swooped up happily, and the dog looked at Sam with eyes that were at once delighted and cautious. It picked up its feet in a dainty way, flipping them back with each step, and carefully made its way through a thicket of legs to the park entrance.

Sam stared as the dog disappeared from sight. His anger began to melt away. He would have sworn that the dog lifted its lip and smiled at him as it went by. I wonder where the bag of buns came from? Sam asked himself and he began to chuckle.

"The show must go on."

Sam started. The voice in his head seemed loud enough for other people to hear. Or maybe it had come from somebody else. And it sounded like . . .

Sam shook his head, feeling silly even thinking that it could have been his uncle's voice.

Regardless, the voice was right. The show *must* go on—in spite of the lost half-dollar coin.

Squaring his shoulders, acting more sure of himself than he felt, Sam walked toward the park's entrance and joined a stream of murmuring people that flowed through.

Once inside the gate, he stopped, feeling like a boulder in a stream as people made their way around him. From the place where he stood the park's rolling gardens stretched down to a glittering, winding river. Bushes seemed to sag under the weight of the sunlight pouring over them, and the grass at his feet looked as if it had been washed, brushed, and left out to dry. He closed his eyes and breathed in the smell of flowers and cut grass. He smiled again, wondering where the dog had taken its bag of goodies, imagining it ripping open the plastic and nibbling at the buns inside.

Opening his eyes, he felt tingly and nervous. He remembered asking his uncle once if he ever felt nervous before doing a show. His uncle had nodded. "Yes," he'd said excitedly. "And it feels *gr-r-reat!*"

Now Sam felt great, as if every part of his body

had been rubbed hard with a huge towel. He was about to perform magic! But first he wanted to organize himself, to make sure that everything in his pockets was where he thought it was. After finding the quarters in mysterious pockets, he didn't know what he'd find in there now. He felt as if the jacket was playing tricks of its own—on him.

Sam walked to a nearby bench and sat. He stuck his hands into the jacket pockets, feeling carefully. There were so many pockets within pockets hidden there! Suddenly the bench trembled. Startled, he turned to see a young woman settling onto the other end of the bench. She was holding the wrist of a three-year-old boy who was trying to pull away from her and was yelling "No! No! No!" at the top of his lungs.

"Come on, Ralph," she said when the child stopped yelling to gulp air. "Let's sit down and rest a moment." But the furious three-year-old closed his eyes and continued to yell, his face turning almost as red as his T-shirt.

Ralph was getting on Sam's nerves. He was about to get up quietly and sneak away when the young woman looked over to him. "Sorry," she said, leaning toward Sam so that he could hear her over the little boy's yelling. She shrugged her shoulders and smiled in a tired way.

Sam nodded politely. "That's O.K.," he said, but not meaning it. Feeling that it would be rude now to get up and leave, he leaned back and tried to concentrate on what was in his jacket pockets. It was hard to do. Ralph got louder and louder. And Sam noticed that the people walking by turned to stare at Ralph and the young woman—and at *him*. Turning a little away from Ralph and the young woman, Sam once again began to check his magic tricks. He reached into the jacket pockets up to his elbows and worked his way backward. His cards were . . . there. And his sponge balls were . . .

The young woman interrupted him and he looked up to her with a sigh. "I don't think I will be baby-sitting Ralph again." She tried to sound perky, but the strain of having Ralph yelling and pulling at her pinched the ends of her smile.

"I bet," Sam said, leaning toward her so that he wouldn't have to shout.

She nodded. "They pay a ton . . . twice what anybody else pays. But I don't think it's worth it. In fact, right now I'd pay them. . . ." She lifted her eyebrows and looked at Ralph.

Ralph, noticing for the first time that he didn't have the baby-sitter's full attention, had suddenly stopped screaming and had turned around to see what was going on. His mouth formed a wonderfully flabby pout that almost made Sam laugh. Ralph looked angrily at his baby-sitter and then glared at Sam.

The baby-sitter smiled. "Well, now. That's better." As she relaxed her hold on Ralph's wrist, the boy snatched his hand away and jammed it into his armpit, locking it down with his arm in case she tried to get it back.

"And what brings you to the park today?" the young woman asked, turning back to Sam. It was an adult kind of question, one that sounded older than she looked.

A proud smile spread across Sam's face. "I'm here to perform magic."

"Magic?" She looked puzzled. "Well, that's . . . interesting. I don't think I've ever seen someone do magic before . . . except on television. Do you have a name . . . you know, a magician's name?"

Sam's excitement drooped. He wished now that he'd figured out a name ahead of time. And then, all at once, much to his amazement, he said, "Excyclamazing Sam." As soon as he said it, he liked the way it sounded.

"Well, well, well," the young woman said, sitting back and folding her arms across her chest. "Excyclamazing Sam. That's a . . . a nice name." She stole a quick glance at Ralph, who was staring at Sam as if he were something disgusting to eat. "If you wouldn't mind, I'd love to see some magic. Wouldn't you, Ralph?"

"No," Ralph said, stamping his feet farther apart in case she tried to pull him next to her.

"Suit yourself." She looked back to Sam. "You wouldn't mind, would you?"

"No," Sam said, swallowing. He hadn't planned to do magic quite like this. He remembered his daydream—standing on a bench, a crowd of admiring people at his feet.

The show must go on, he heard in his head again.

The young woman looked pleased and relieved. Ralph turned so that his shoulder was pointing toward Sam. Even so, Sam could tell that Ralph was watching him out of the corner of an eye.

With a flick of his wrist, Sam slipped his hand inside his jacket, reaching for his magic scarf—the same one that Uncle Frank had given to him on his fifth birthday, a little raggedy now but as impressive as ever.

Holding on to it in just the right way, but not yet taking it out of the pocket, Sam cleared his throat. He felt nervous and he was surprised by how wonderful it felt.

Taking a deep breath, Sam hoped his voice would sound like his uncle's. Then, without warning, he twirled around and looked over at the woman. "Lady . . ."—and then he looked at Ralph, whose head was turned toward him and immediately snapped away again—" . . . and gentleman! Today you will see exciting and amazing things . . . things you have only seen in your wildest dreams."

Sam felt terrific. He didn't know where the magic was coming from, but it was coming from someplace—he could feel it.

Pulling out the scarf, he ignored Ralph. "This," he said, waving the cloth as if it were a flag, "may look like a regular scarf. But things are not always what they seem to be. This scarf was given to me by Phantasmagoric Frank, my uncle and the greatest magician who ever lived. This scarf has fantastic powers." Words whistled dramatically through the gap in his teeth.

The young woman smiled, collecting her hands in her lap and pressing her ankles together. Sam bowed slightly to her and held the scarf by one corner, letting the rest of it dangle. "Ma'am, would you tell me what color this scarf is?"

Before she could answer, Ralph shouted, "Red!"

Sam tipped his head toward Ralph but still refused to look at the boy. "Right you are. A red scarf, but with powers that are greater than any scarf you have ever seen before." He picked up the dangling end of the scarf and brought his hands together.

"Watch closely," he said, lowering his voice mysteriously and finally looking Ralph in the eye. "The magic word is *abracadabra*. If we say it together, we can make the magic work."

"Abra . . ." Sam began.

"Ca-daba," Ralph shouted, overpowering Sam's voice.

Sam pulled his hands apart and let go of one end of the scarf. There, hanging from his hand, was a yellow scarf.

Ralph's jaw dropped and his eyes bulged. The young woman laughed and began to clap.

"But wait," Sam said, holding up his free hand. The woman stopped clapping and pressed her hands together. "If you were a red scarf, how would you like to be suddenly turned yellow?" He picked up the dangling end and brought his hands together. "You'd feel terrible, of course. But look! We can change this yellow scarf back with the magic word. . . ."

"Aba-daba-daba!" Ralph shouted.

Sam pulled his hands apart. Again Ralph stared at the red scarf, not believing his eyes.

"What a relief it must be for this red scarf to be red. Now it can be put back where it came from, safe and sound." Sam wadded up the scarf and stuffed it into the pocket from which it came. He bowed as the young lady began to clap again.

"Again!" Ralph shouted. "Do again! 'gen, 'gen, 'gen, 'gen!" He jumped up and down in his excitement.

"I'm so glad you asked. One more trick for Ralph." Sam reached into his pocket and felt around for the quarter he'd found earlier. Grabbing it tightly so that it wouldn't slip into some other hidden pocket along the way, he drew it out and held it in front of Ralph's nose, so close Ralph had to cross his eyes to see. "As you can see, this is an ordinary quarter . . . good anywhere for some bubble gum or a piece of candy."

"Gimme," said Ralph, grabbing for the quarter. Just in time Sam closed his hand around it and put both of his hands behind his back. He arranged the quarter into its proper position in his left hand and brought both hands forward. "As you can see, I have a quarter in my left hand. But not for long." He reached over with his right hand, seeming to take the quarter, which instead fell into the cupped palm of his left hand. He closed both hands as he pulled the right hand toward Ralph.

"Touch my hand, Ralph, and say the magic word."

Ralph reached out, paused, and touched Sam's hand quickly, as if it were red hot. "Aca-daba-baba!"

With a flourish, Sam opened the hand Ralph had touched. "Ralph! You made the quarter disappear!"

"Gimme!" Ralph yelled, feeling tricked and not liking it very much.

"But what is this?" Sam reached his left hand to Ralph's neck. Quickly, before Ralph could see, he shoved the quarter with his thumb toward his finger tips. Making his face look surprised, he brought the quarter around so Ralph could see. "It was in your ear!" he said, looking at Ralph's shocked face.

Sam looked over to see if Ralph's baby-sitter had

been fooled too. At that moment Ralph snatched the quarter from Sam's hand. "Mine!" Ralph yelled, spinning around and running down the path.

"Oh dear," the baby-sitter said.

"That's my bus money!" He took a step to run after Ralph when the baby-sitter stood and put a hand on his shoulder. For the first time, Sam noticed how much taller she was than he was.

"Don't. Please. He'll be impossible if you take it away from him." She dug into a pocket and handed him two quarters. "Here. They gave me way too much for lunch. And thanks. It was worth it."

She looked down the path toward the disappearing Ralph. "Guess I'd better go catch him," she said with a sigh, "whether I want to or not."

She trotted down the path, but after a few steps she stopped and turned around. "Hey, maybe I'll see you on TV some day." And then she waved before spinning around and chasing Ralph.

Every time Uncle Frank came for a visit he brought Sam some coins in a little drawstring leather pouch. The coins were always special. Usually they were American coins. Sometimes they were foreign coins— greenish Israeli coins with holes in the middle, or aluminum coins from France. But whether they were American or foreign, whether they were pennies or shekels *or* centimes, *they all had one thing in com-*

mon: They bore the number of the year Sam was born.

Uncle Frank always waited until he tucked Sam into bed before he'd make the pouch seem to appear out of thin air. Sam and Uncle Frank would examine each coin before dropping it into the cookie jar Sam kept by his bed. Uncle Frank would tell him anything that was unusual about the coin—what country it came from, what he was about to buy with it until he noticed the date, if it was a coin he'd found on a street and where that street was.

And then, when Sam was five, the cookie jar filled up so much that the lid wouldn't sit properly. He asked his mother what to do, and one afternoon she helped him sort out the foreign coins from the American coins. "Sam, I think we should take this money to the bank," she said, pointing to the American coins.

Sam squinted, not certain that he liked her idea. He'd been to the bank many times before, and it was a dreary place where people walked around as if they were scared of something.

"We could set up a savings account, one of your very own," his mother continued. "Your money would be safe. And it would earn interest."

Sam liked the idea of his money being safe. "What's interest?" he asked.

♥

"Well . . ." His mother thought for a moment. "It's when the people at the bank borrow your money, and then when they replace it, they put in a few more coins than they borrowed."

"Why do they borrow my money?" Sam asked. He didn't like the idea of people touching his money at all, except maybe his mother and father. And Uncle Frank, of course.

"Oh, I . . . Well, they find things to . . ." She looked at Sam's face and decided to start over. "When you earn interest, it's as if your money . . . it's as if your money has babies." She smiled, pleased with this thought. "If you put in ten pennies, after a year or so one of them has a baby and you have eleven pennies instead of ten."

"Do nickels have babies too?" Sam asked, wondering if baby coins were just like their parents, or if they were smaller.

His mother nodded. "Yes. And dimes and quarters."

Sam smiled. The next time Uncle Frank visited, he could show him the baby coins.

A few days later Sam and his mother went to the bank with his coins in a plastic bag made for hot dog buns. The teller let him come behind the counter to watch her pour his coins into a big, loud, clanking machine that separated them into pennies, nickels, dimes, and quarters and, at the same time, counted them. He was proud of the little savings booklet that the teller gave him with the total amount of the money he'd put in the bank.

Sam's mother kept the savings booklet in her purse. Sometimes he wished he had his coins—to look at or to play with. But then he also liked to think about his coins at the bank having babies.

A couple of months later his mother announced that Uncle Frank was going to visit. He immediately thought of the coins his uncle would give him and the coins in the bank.

"Do you think it's enough time for my coins to have babies?" he asked his mother.

She cocked her head to one side and looked at him a moment before she nodded. "Yes," she said. "I think it's been enough time." Before she could say any more Sam ran off, happy with her answer.

The day his uncle was to arrive, Sam's mother went to the bank. He waited patiently while his mother and the teller did their business, wishing that he was tall enough to see over the top of the counter.

When his mother was done and had stepped aside,

♣

putting her money away, he tugged on her purse.

"Could I have my savings book?" he asked.

"Sure. Did you bring some coins to deposit?" She began rummaging around in her purse.

"I want to get my coins out. And the babies too."

A dark look passed over his mother's face as she looked at him. "Why?" she asked.

"To show Uncle Frank."

Sam's mother took her hand from her purse and reached down for his hand. "Let's go home, honey. I think I have to explain something to you." She kept her voice just above a whisper.

"I want my coins," he said loudly, planting his feet apart and pulling his arms into a knot behind his back. "I want them . . . now.*"*

"Sam, let's go.*" His mother's voice was low but firm and she held his shoulder tightly as she guided him out the door. He made her work for every step he took.*

When they got into the car, his mother helped him buckle up and then sat for a minute, holding the steering wheel and looking out the windshield, even though they weren't going anyplace.

"Sam," she finally said, and then nibbled at her lower lip as she thought for a moment. "Did you expect

the teller to give you back the very same coins you put into the bank?"

He nodded.

"I think I made a terrible mistake then." She reached over and patted his thigh. "You see, Sam, I'm afraid that you won't get back the very same coins you put into the bank."

"Uncle Frank gave me those coins," Sam pointed out, feeling angry.

"I know, honey. And I feel awful about it. I didn't realize . . ." She sighed. "This is terrible. Just terrible."

Sam was quiet as they drove home. He wanted his coins back. And if his mother couldn't help him, then Uncle Frank could. He made things disappear all the time. And he sometimes made them appear again. He knew that his uncle could make his coins appear—the very same coins he put in the bank.

Uncle Frank arrived just before bedtime. As his uncle tucked him in, Sam told him what had happened to the coins and about the baby coins that he knew were in the bank. "And I want you to use magic to get them out of the bank," he said.

A pained look came into Uncle Frank's eyes and he

♥

shook his head. "Magic doesn't work like that, Sam. I'm afraid I can't get your coins back."

"I want *my coins back. They have my birthday on them. I want the bank to give them to me . . . and their babies too."*

His chest began to heave. Sam had been so sure Uncle Frank could help.

"I just can't make them do that," his uncle said. "Let's look at the coins I brought this time."

Sam had never been angry with his uncle before. "I want my coins back!" he yelled.

"Sam, I'm sorry about the coins. But they're gone." His uncle looked and sounded sad. "I can't bring them back with my magic. There's nothing I can do."

Uncle Frank pulled Sam close and patted him on the back while Sam cried. And when he finished crying, Uncle Frank wiped off Sam's face.

"We'll just have to start over again," Uncle Frank said. "Well now! Would you just look what just popped out of your ear. Feel it?" Sam felt an itch as his uncle reached up to his ear and pulled back the pouch. He sniffled and smiled at his uncle to be polite, not because he was happy.

Uncle Frank poured the coins onto Sam's bed and began telling Sam about each one. And when he came to a nickel he picked it up and said, "Ah, this is a special coin. I remember this one."

Sam stared at it, trying to see if it was different in some way.

"Here," his uncle said. "Put it in your hand and squeeze it as hard as you can." His uncle placed it in Sam's hand and helped him make a fist. "Squeeze harder, harder, harder! Don't be afraid. You won't hurt it."

Sam closed his eyes and squeezed everything in his body—his mouth, his legs, his eyelids, his jaw, his toes, his hand—squeezed everything as hard as he could.

"Now," his uncle said, "open your hand."

Sam had squeezed so hard that he had to struggle to open his hand. But when he did, he gasped.

In his hand, where the nickel should have been, were five stacked pennies. The stack tipped over and Sam looked closer. Each one bore the date of his birth!

"Someday you'll have to show me how you did that trick," Uncle Frank said, winking at him.

5

The park was wonderfully quiet with Ralph gone. Even the birds seemed to enjoy the silence for a moment before chirping again.

The day was growing hotter, the lid of sky pressing tighter and tighter. Sam looked at the quarters in his hand and thought about ice cream. Licking his lips, he pictured in his mind a little kiosk toward the center of the park.

He now had one quarter for bus fare and, thanks to Ralph, an extra quarter for anything he wanted. Sam couldn't remember exactly how much an ice cream cone cost, but he knew it was more than a quarter. Even so, he decided to give it a try. Maybe, if the kiosk wasn't busy, he could talk the man inside into giving him a dab of ice cream—whatever amounted to a quarter's worth—or get the man to sell him a snow cone with a quarter's worth of syrup.

He stood and slipped the quarters into the good pocket of his jeans. Trees arched overhead as he walked from shade puddle to shade puddle, zig-zagging down the sidewalk. He rounded a corner and there was the kiosk, right where he knew it would be. A long line of people stretched out from the kiosk's open window. The kiosk sat in the sun, away from any trees or shade, and the people in the line looked miserable.

He stood for a moment, thinking, letting his tongue play with the gap where his tooth had been. The line was moving slowly. It would take him a long time to inch from the back to the front. And with such a big line, he didn't think he'd have much luck talking the man in the kiosk into giving him a quarter's worth of ice cream. But even so, he was hungry enough to give it a try and he walked to the end of the line.

The sun beat down and the air sat heavily on his shoulders. The line crept forward and Sam shuffled until he was near the middle. He studied the man in the kiosk. It didn't look promising. The man had a face like a rock—a pebble nose and a chin that looked chipped and cracked. He never smiled or talked. Instead, the man nodded when an order was given to him and nodded again when he handed out the ice cream or snow cone or soda or chips in one hand while taking the money in the other hand.

"Hey, Mommy." Sam heard a kid's voice behind him. "Why is that boy wearing funny clothes?"

"Now, Sarah . . ." Sam heard a warning in the woman's voice.

He looked ahead of him, wondering who in the line was wearing funny clothes. Nobody that he could see. And then he felt someone tugging on the back of his jacket.

"Sarah! What did I tell you?"

Sam turned and looked down at Sarah, who was looking at him with big eyes. She was talking about him!

He looked up at the woman who was scolding Sarah. "Sarah, that is rude. You mustn't do that again." He decided that she had to be Sarah's mother.

"That's O.K.," he said, smiling first at Sarah's mother and then at Sarah. He looked down at the jacket. It *was* a little odd, especially in this heat.

"Why are you wearing it?" Sarah asked. Her mother sighed, closed her eyes, and tipped her face to the sky.

"Because," he said, feeling so proud that for a moment he forgot how hot it was, "I'm a magician and this is a magician's jacket."

Sarah was impressed. Sam reached into his jacket pockets, located the sponge balls with his fingertips, and decided to use only one of them. And then he looked at Sarah. "I'm . . ."—Sam drew himself up even taller, and his voice grew bigger— ". . . Excyclamazing Sam!" He pulled the sponge ball from his pocket.

"Sarah," he said, kneeling partway so that she didn't have to look up at him quite so much. "I need someone special to help me do my magic, someone who believes in magic. Do you believe in magic?"

Sarah blinked with excitement as she nodded.

"So do I." He glanced at Sarah's mother. Her arms were folded across her chest but she was smiling pleasantly enough as she watched. He noticed that several people in back of her were watching too.

Swallowing a lump of nervousness, Sam held a ball with the thumb and fingers of his right hand.

"I'm going to place the ball in my left hand," he said, placing the ball in his left palm and closing that hand over his right hand. Pulling his right hand away he thrust his left hand closer to Sarah. "Now, Sarah, I'd like for you to touch my hand and lend me some of your magic by saying the magic word. . . ."

"Abracadabra," they said together. Sam slowly turned his hand over, opening his fingers at the same time. It was empty and Sarah gasped.

"But look at this!" Sam reached his right hand up to Sarah's ear and drew back the sponge ball, which he'd pushed toward his fingertips with his thumb.

A couple of people in back of Sarah clapped.

"Wow!" Sarah breathed in as she spoke.

Sam looked over his shoulder and saw that the line had moved quite a bit while he did that trick and that he was near the front. Taking a couple of steps backward, he turned to Sarah, so pleased with himself and his magic that he didn't want to stop. He wanted to keep doing magic as long as he could. "Would you like to see another trick, Sarah? A quick one?" He stuck the sponge ball into the pocket with the others.

Sarah nodded eagerly.

He pulled the regular deck of cards out of his other jacket pocket, knelt, and began to shuffle them on his thigh. "A long time ago an old magician was shuffling his cards when. . ." The leg he was shuffling on began to tighten and cramp. He shifted his weight to relax it and lost his balance.

"Whoa!" he gasped, throwing his hands up to steady himself. Cards rained down onto the cement with a splattering sound.

"*Frigate!*" Sam said, forcing the word out of the gap in his teeth. He dropped to his hands and knees and began picking up cards. Sam and Sarah bumped heads reaching for the same card.

"I beg your pardon. What did you say?"

Sam looked up at Sarah's mother, surprised by the scolding tone in her voice. And then he understood.

"Oh, that. Sometimes when I'm angry I say *frigate,*" Sam said. "It's a kind of ship," he explained.

Sarah's mother squinted at him.

A man behind her piped up. "Ever seen a frigate, son?"

Sam shook his head.

"Moved like clouds across the water." The man walked around Sarah's mother and stooped next to Sam. "Here. Let me help."

The person in front of Sam helped too and, when it was his turn he handed the cards he'd collected to Sam.

"Thanks. Thanks a lot. Thanks. Thank you," Sam muttered, trying to sound polite as people handed him cards. Picking up the last card, Sam stood and turned to face the kiosk.

He jammed the cards every which way in a jacket pocket and stepped up to the window. He hesitated for a moment, not knowing exactly how to ask what he wanted to ask. "I wonder if I could have a quarter's worth of ice cream? Chocolate chip, please."

To his surprise, the man in the kiosk didn't argue or get rude. Instead, he nodded and reached for a cone and the ice cream scoop. Sam watched as the man's hand disappeared into a tub that sat in a freezer and carved out a huge ball of ice cream. The man placed the ball onto the cone, pressed it down, and reached for more.

Frigate, Sam thought. He didn't understand me. And when he finds out I only have a quarter, he's going to be angry.

"Sir," Sam said, standing on his toes and leaning as far into the kiosk as he could. "I don't think you heard me. . . ."

The man pressed the second large ball of ice cream onto the first and handed the cone to Sam.

"I heard," the man said, his voice surprisingly soft for such a rough face. Sam held out the quarter and the man put a finger to his lips and leaned toward Sam. "Put that back in your pocket. This is already paid for. Double or nothing. Take it or leave it." The man smiled stiffly.

"Th-th-thanks," Sam stammered, most of the word whistling through the gap in his teeth. He stepped aside and watched as Sarah grabbed hold of the window's lower edge, pulling herself up off the ground, high enough so that she could see inside.

"I want the same as what Excyclamazing Sam got." And then Sarah's fingers slipped off the ledge and she dropped to the ground. Looking up at Sam, she smiled.

"See ya," he said to Sarah as he turned around.

The ice cream was melting fast as he walked toward shade and tried to lick away the streams that slid toward his hand. Sitting on a bench, he held the cone out almost at arm's length to keep it from dripping onto his jeans. He leaned over the ice cream, turning the cone around in his hand so that he got all sides. He licked as fast as he could, but ice cream trickled down his hands and made a growing puddle between his feet.

And then, seeming to come from nowhere, the yellow dog he'd seen earlier with the bag of buns appeared, nuzzled in between his knees, and began licking the ice cream puddle. Sam continued to race the trickling ice cream and grinned as he watched the drips land on the dog's head—right between the ears.

When the puddle was nothing more than a damp spot on the pavement, the dog sat a polite distance away and watched Sam finish the ice cream. As Sam popped the last of the cone into his mouth, the dog pulled in his tongue, swallowed, and cocked his head.

"That's it," Sam said, holding up his hands and wiggling all ten fingers. "Magic. I made it disappear."

All business, the dog got up and trotted off, his tail curved up into a lopsided smile.

Uncle Frank was always practicing magic—when he watched television, as he talked on the phone, sometimes even at dinner. "There's never enough time to practice," he sometimes said. "I wish I could practice when I sleep. I wish I could practice ten things at once."

Sam loved to watch his uncle practice.

Uncle Frank seemed to have certain things he prac-

ticed at certain times. While he watched television, he would often weave a coin between his fingers, moving it over and under as it went from his little finger to his forefinger and back again. The coin seemed to move on its own, diving down and popping up, slipping between his uncle's fingers faster and faster, his fingers barely moving.

Sam watched very little television while his uncle practiced coin weaving—especially when his uncle would weave two coins, one in each hand.

While on the telephone, his uncle sometimes practiced shuffling cards with whichever hand was free. As he chatted, he might pull a single card from the deck, flip it over, and then return it to the bottom. Or he might divide the deck in two and flip the two halves around and then back together again.

While he ate, Uncle Frank sometimes practiced making a thimble disappear with his left hand. Even though Sam had never seen him use thimbles in his magic act, his uncle said that they made him especially aware of his fingertips.

At dinner one night Sam's mother tried to ignore Uncle Frank's left hand as it worked away beside his plate, making the thimble appear and disappear faster

♥

and faster. Finally she couldn't stand it any longer. "I hate to sound like a prude," she said, "but your thimble is driving me crazy."

"Sorry," Uncle Frank said.

But that didn't stop him. He just moved his left hand to his lap and continued practicing there—which drove Sam crazy. He pictured the thimble moving from finger to palm, appearing and disappearing from thumb or finger. During the rest of dinner Sam dropped his napkin onto the floor as many times as he dared so that he could peek at his uncle's thimble practice.

Uncle Frank's last visit went by faster than any visit Sam could remember. And when the time came, Sam didn't want him to leave. He was feeling sad, not knowing what to say as he and Uncle Frank sat outside on the front steps waiting for a taxi to take Uncle Frank to the airport.

As usual, his uncle was practicing—this time a coin trick that Sam had never seen before: He made a quarter go right through the back of his hand and out the other side.

"What do you call that trick?" Sam asked, looking up from his uncle's hands to his uncle's face. He'd noticed that during this visit Uncle Frank looked tired

most of the time, especially around the eyes. *Right now, in the afternoon light, his uncle's eyes were sunken and dark, as if he'd rubbed them with dirty hands.*

"I call it the passing-the-coin-through-the-hand-so-that-people-stop-and-stare trick," his uncle said. *When he grinned, his eyes didn't look so tired.*

"Aw, come on," Sam said, bumping against his uncle's arm with his shoulder. "I bet you have a better name than that when you do it in front of people."

"You're right," Uncle Frank said. "I call it the stabbing-yourself-in-the-hand-with-a-quarter-so-hard-that-you-don't-even-bleed trick."

"Uncle Frank!" Sam smiled. *He saw his uncle begin to put the quarter in his pants pocket.* "Would you do it again?"

Uncle Frank's eyebrows raised as he looked at Sam. "You know that a magician should never repeat a trick before the same audience."

"Please?" *He wanted to see if he could figure out what his uncle had been doing.*

"You're sure?" *his uncle asked.* "You know, seeing it again could take the fun out of it." *He frowned.* "People who watch magic shouldn't mind being tricked. Do you mind?"

♣

"Sometimes," Sam said. "And sometimes I like being tricked." His uncle seemed pleased with his answer, so in his most wheedling voice Sam asked, "Again? Please?" He sat back and waited, certain that his uncle would do what he wanted.

"Oh, all right." Uncle Frank sighed. "Watch carefully."

Sam watched his uncle tap the quarter onto the back of his hand two times. His uncle quickly showed him that the palm of the hand he had tapped was empty. Turning the hand over, he tapped its back again, hard.

This time, when he turned his hand around, the quarter lay in his palm. Uncle Frank showed Sam the hand that had held the quarter so that he would know that this hand was empty also.

Sam was completely fooled, but he tried not to show it. "Could I see the quarter?" he asked.

"Sure." His uncle handed him the quarter. He saw that it was real, not fake, and handed it back.

"Would you do it again?"

"Again?" This time his uncle didn't sound so pleased.

"Pretty please?"

Without another word, his mouth a thin line, Uncle Frank quickly repeated the trick once more. Sam

♠

watched carefully and he thought he caught a glimpse of how his uncle did it.

"Could you . . ."

"Again?" His uncle looked down at him with narrowed eyes.

"Just once more. One more time and that's it," Sam pleaded. "I won't ask again. I promise."

"Once more, then."

Again Sam looked carefully, especially at the point in the trick when he thought his uncle slipped the coin into his palm.

"O.K." Uncle Frank handed the quarter to Sam. "Now you do it."

"Naw." He was suddenly embarrassed. "I think I know how to do it, but I need to practice."

A battered taxi came down the street and stopped in front of the house. The exhaust pipe rattled and shook as the engine rumbled and wheezed. The driver honked his horn several times and Uncle Frank waved to signal that he was coming.

"All right." Uncle Frank grunted as he stood. "The next time I visit, I expect you to show me that trick, O.K.?" He reached into a pocket. "And here's another quarter," he said, smiling at Sam, "in case the first

♥

one gets stuck in your hand halfway through.”

“Gross,” Sam said, taking the quarter and giving his uncle a hug.

His uncle picked up his suitcase and walked down the sidewalk to the taxi—more slowly than Sam had ever seen him walk before.

6

Sam's fingers were stiff with dried up, melted ice cream. He'd never be able to do magic tricks with such sticky fingers, so he popped each one into his mouth, licking and sucking until he could no longer taste ice cream.

He saved his thumbs for last, thinking that people walking by would find it odd to see a boy his age sucking a thumb. Just as he was finishing, he heard someone yell from across the plaza, from the left of the kiosk.

"Hey kid!" Sam quickly took his thumb out of his mouth. He looked toward the sound.

"Yeah, you! The magician. Come here!"

Sam squinted into the brightness beyond the

shade where he was sitting. And then he saw the person who was yelling: an older boy, maybe high school, with an arm around a girl whose short blond hair sat on her head like a golden helmet, gleaming in the sun.

The boy waved for him to come over. He looked friendly enough, so Sam wiped his damp fingers on his jeans and walked over to the boy and girl.

"Hi," Sam said, standing in front of them. He began to sweat and he wondered why they were sitting in the sun when they could be sitting in the shade.

"Hi, yourself," the boy said, taking his arm off the girl's shoulder.

"Hello," the girl said, smiling at Sam in a shy kind of way.

"I watched you do a trick back there with that sponge thing," the boy said, leaning forward and putting his elbows on his knees. "You looked real good."

Sam thought he heard mischief in the boy's voice, but he couldn't be sure. He hadn't been around older boys that much and he decided that that was probably just the way they talked. "Thanks," he said, slipping his hands into his jacket pockets.

"You been studying magic long?" The boy had

a smile that just wouldn't stop. He found himself looking at the boy's white teeth instead of listening to what he was saying.

"Huh?" Sam looked up to the boy's eyes. "Oh, yeah. I've been studying for about a month . . . or so."

"That's great!" The boy smiled toward the girl and then back at Sam. "You perform your magic often? You know, in public?"

Sam shook his head. "This is the first time." He was beginning to feel uncomfortable and more of his words were whistling through the gap in his teeth than usual.

"Well, I liked what I saw back there." The boy sat back and reached into a pants pocket. He sounded like a hotshot. "And I thought you could help me with a little trick I've been practicing. You know, coach me a little."

"I didn't know you could do magic," the girl said, leaning away so that she got a better look at the boy's face.

"Yeah, well, I do a little magic now and then." The boy smiled. His face suddenly grew serious as he leaned farther back, searching first one pocket and then the other.

"Oh dear," he said, looking up at Sam with unhappy eyes. "I need a couple of quarters for this trick and I guess I just don't have any."

His girlfriend pulled her purse close and reached inside. But Sam was faster. He popped his hand out of his pocket and held out the quarters. "Here," he said, relieved that the quarters were still there.

The boy smiled. "Thanks." He sat up and his eyes were happy now. Sam didn't like the way they changed moods so fast.

The girl looked up, saw Sam's quarters, and stopped searching her purse. She turned around so that she could see her boyfriend's magic trick.

The boy took Sam's quarters and looked at them. "I think these will do," he said, poking them with a finger. His smile grew larger. "Now, the trick I do is making quarters disappear."

Sam tipped his head to one side. There were several ways to make coins disappear and he wondered which one this boy would use.

"Now watch closely," the boy said. "Abracadabra, please and thank you." And then with a flourish, he leaned back and stuck them deep into his pocket. Taking out his empty hand, he held it in front of Sam's face. "Ta-da!" he sang, laughing.

Sam's eyes widened and then quickly narrowed. "Now wait a minute. . . ." Sam didn't like being made a fool of. He almost told the boy to give him back his money but decided he didn't want to beg, which was just what the boy wanted him to do. Sam hated that—big kids making little kids beg. Clamping his mouth shut, he stared at the boy hatefully, turned, and stomped away.

"George. . . ." Sam heard surprise and anger in the girl's voice. "I don't think that was nice. You give that boy back his money. You give it back or . . . or I'll walk home."

Sam slowed down, listening hard.

"Jeeze," he heard George whine. "It was just a joke. I wasn't going to keep the kid's money. What do you think I am, anyway?"

"I don't know," the girl said.

"Hey, kid." Sam kept walking. "Hey, kid! Don't walk away mad. I didn't mean anything."

Sam kept walking. He wasn't going back until George begged—a big kid begging a small kid. He liked the idea of that.

"Good-bye, George." The girl sounded almost as angry as Sam felt.

"Hey, kid. Come back. Please. Please come on back. Hey! I'm begging you!"

Sam stopped and turned around slowly. George was standing and digging around in his pockets for money. He pulled out a handful of coins. "Here. Jeeze! Can't you take a joke?" He really did look sorry. He turned to his girlfriend. "Come on, Beth, don't be angry. I wasn't going to take the kid's money. I was going to give it back."

Beth looked up, her sharp stare poking at his face. And then she looked at Sam. "Is that O.K. with you?" she asked.

Sam nodded and stepped up to George, who dumped the change into his hand. It was warm, and mostly pennies with a crumpled silver gum wrapper thrown in. Sitting on top were his two quarters.

Beth's face brightened. "Good." She looked at Sam. "Could you do a couple of tricks for us? That first trick you did in the line was neat."

Sam thought for a moment. He was still sore at George and he didn't know if he felt like doing a trick for him or not. But this girl was nice, and there was one trick he hadn't yet done in front of an audience, a trick he wanted to do before he went home—a trick for his uncle.

"Sure." He picked a quarter out from the change and slipped the rest of the coins into a pants pocket—the one without the hole.

The man who'd been in line behind Sam, the

one who knew what a frigate was, walked up to them. "Gonna do a magic show?" he asked. He looked at the coin in Sam's hand. "Costs a quarter?" Not waiting for an answer, he handed Sam a quarter.

"Thanks," Sam said.

"Just a second," the man said. He handed Sam a second quarter. "Let me get my wife."

He suddenly felt more nervous than he'd ever felt before. His stomach felt as if he'd eaten a jar of pickles. Being this nervous didn't feel as good as being a little nervous.

To calm himself, Sam faced the bench for a few minutes, straightening out the cards that had scattered in the kiosk line and making sure the scarf was in the right place and that the sponge balls hadn't fallen into a pocket within a pocket that he didn't even know he had.

When he turned around, he was surprised to see almost a dozen people gathered around. His heart beat in his throat and he swallowed several times to steady himself.

Holding the quarter in his right hand he climbed onto the bench and cleared his throat. He remembered to turn on a smile, knowing that it wasn't a relaxed easy smile but it was a smile nonetheless.

"Ladies and gentlemen!" He looked around the group of people who were looking up at him. A trickle of sweat ran down his cheek, warm as a tear. He ignored it. "Today you will see exciting and amazing things . . . things you have only seen in your wildest dreams." Sam noticed a couple of people join the back of the crowd. Everybody was looking up at him and he liked the way their smiles made him feel. He took a deep breath. "I'm Excyclamazing Sam, and I got my magic from the most amazing magician in the world: Phantasmagoric Frank."

Sam felt wonderful. He could feel the magic. His uncle had been right. He could feel the magic coming from the people who were watching him, coming from their eyes and their smiles.

Holding out the quarter for everybody to see, Sam continued. "This . . . is an ordinary quarter. Look carefully as I tap the quarter onto the back of my hand."

Everybody's eyes shifted to the back of Sam's hand. Sam's eyes shifted too. And when he looked up, he gasped, staring at the back of the group of people.

Standing in the back, red in the face, and looking very cross indeed, was Mrs. Goodman. And next to her, jumping up and down so that he could see over the heads of the people in front of him, was Charles—with a porcupine-style haircut that was so ugly it was almost funny.

Sam snapped his eyes forward and looked into Beth's eyes. She smiled encouragement at him. He fanned out his left hand to show everybody that it was empty. "And now . . ."—his voice was unsteady and he coughed quickly and continued— ". . . watch carefully as I *force* . . ."—Sam grunted as he hit the back of his hand one last time— ". . . this quarter through my own flesh and blood."

Quickly Sam opened his left hand, showing the quarter lying on his palm. At the same time, he held up his right hand to show that it was empty. A few people began to clap, and soon everyone else joined in. Pleased, Sam looked up, avoiding the spot where Mrs. Goodman stood.

But he couldn't help seeing Charles. His best friend was smiling his beaver smile and jumping up and down.

"Frigate," he muttered, as he looked behind Charles. His legs almost buckled.

At the very back of the crowd he saw his mother and father.

Since Uncle Frank died, Sam had dreamed of him only once.

The dream began with Sam dressed in a top hat and a suit with tails that reached all the way to his heels. And he was standing in front of a mirror that was as big as a bedroom door, practicing the quarter-through-the-hand trick. He was finally getting it, moving so skillfully that he could barely see the quarter when he slipped it into his left palm before he closed the hand.

"One more time," he told his other self in the mirror. He smiled and noticed that, for the first time, his other self didn't smile when he did. Instead, his other self was frowning. "Come on," Sam said, crossing his arms and looking at his other self, angry that the boy in the mirror wasn't imitating him. "I can't practice without you." His other self just stared off to the side, ignoring him.

"Listen, buddy," Sam leaned forward and talked loudly into the glassy ear of his other self. "Hey, I know this is boring. Practice, practice, practice. Over and over and over again. But look, I want to do this trick for Uncle Frank when he comes back and I need your help to practice." The boy in the mirror just shrugged his shoulders.

Sam was about to poke his other self with a finger, when the boy in the mirror glanced at him with a tense, warning look on his face. And then taking a deep breath, his other self moved into a position that was like Sam's—only floppy and tired and pouty.

Sam tried to ignore the way his other self was acting and began to do the trick again. His other self followed him, about half a heartbeat behind. It was confusing—like talking and hearing a word only when the next one was spoken. But his hands and fingers were remembering more and more, which meant that he didn't need to see what he was doing in the mirror as much as before. His hands and fingers were almost able to do the trick on their own.

Sam had tapped the back of his left hand twice with the quarter and was just about to open his left hand to show that it was empty, when the mirror began to ripple like the disturbed water of a bathtub. Sam blinked, trying to focus his eyes and to stop the mirror from moving. His other self looked frightened, holding its arms out sideways for balance. And then the boy in the mirror disappeared as the waves grew larger and more violent.

Sam gasped as a hand came through the mirror— a large hand with long delicate fingers. His own hand disappeared as the large hand wrapped over and around it, close and tight as cellophane. And then the large hand pulled on his. Sam leaned back, afraid of being pulled inside. Instead, out of the crazy waves in the mirror came Uncle Frank. Streams of watery light ran off his face, and Uncle Frank shook his hair free of the drops of light that clung to each strand. Drops splattered on Sam's face, but they felt dry and powdery, not

♦

the least bit wet, and they disappeared instantly.

"Hello, Sam," his uncle said, smiling. "I've missed you." He looked Sam up and down. "You look terrific, and I couldn't help noticing that you've made some progress with that trick." Uncle Frank put his other hand on Sam's shoulder and Sam felt the coolness of a shadow. "You still need to work on your timing. I can see that quarter slipping into the left hand, oh, I'd say about half the time."

Sam was speechless. He looked at his uncle's eyes— those incredible blue eyes that were so kind and happy and, at the same time, so hard and sad—those eyes that wore his uncle's face like a mask.

"I never said good-bye," his uncle continued. "I don't know when I'll get another chance."

Sam realized he'd been holding his breath. He let it out and with it came a question he'd been holding in also. "Why?"

Uncle Frank nodded, understanding Sam's question perfectly. "I don't know," he answered. "But it happened, didn't it? And I didn't want you to see me near the end."

He felt his uncle's hand letting go of his own. And his uncle's other hand slipped off his shoulder.

"Silly, wasn't it?" his uncle said. "I know that now.

♣

But I was ashamed. I knew that you knew, but I didn't want you to know."

Sam wanted to grab hold of his uncle's hand again, hold it and never let it go. He wanted to hold so tightly that when he woke up his uncle would be there, sitting on the edge of his bed, smiling down on him, just like when he came to visit. But his uncle was beginning to fade. Sam could see through his uncle and he saw the mirror behind begin to stir again, as if a wind were blowing across it, making ripples that roughened into waves.

"Sam, don't ever lose your magic. Don't let anybody take it away from you. Remember something for me, would you?" His uncle spoke faster and faster, as if he was running out of time. "Some people say that seeing is believing. They're right, of course. But I think they forget something that is even more important." His uncle's voice was fading too, sounding farther and farther away. "I always thought that believing is seeing. Believe in magic and you'll see magic. Believe in beauty and you'll see beautiful things. Think about it, O.K.? O.K.? Will you?"

His uncle's face froze in panic and his eyes darted about, looking and not seeing. "Sam? Sam? Sam!"

"Uncle Frank!" Sam cried, as his uncle sank into

♠

the mirror and disappeared like a stone in water. Sam wanted to reach his hand through the waves of light and pull his uncle out but he couldn't move. Slowly the ripples calmed and the mirror grew glassy. At last Sam could see his other self clearly and his other self looked as if he was about to cry.

And for the first time, Sam noticed the eyes in the mirror, the eyes of his other self. He knew those eyes. They were his own.

But they were also the eyes of Uncle Frank looking back at him.

7

Sam was alone in his room now, sitting on the floor, surrounded by the boxes filled with magic tricks. He'd dragged them out from under his bed after Charles left. His room was hot, and a swarm of dust particles from under his bed filled the air, thick and agitated, darting and flashing in the sunlight.

Pulling his uncle's magician's jacket closed in front, Sam gently rocked back and forth to calm himself. He closed his eyes and his throat tightened as if he was going to hum, but no sound came out. His throat felt like a kinked hose, and he let the trapped sound out slowly, in strangled, gurgly spurts.

Sam felt sorry for himself—sorry about his new haircut that made him look as silly as Charles—sorry that his uncle's birthday had ended on such an angry note—sorry about summer vacation being over and school starting tomorrow—sorry that for the first time ever he wouldn't be in the same class as Charles—sorry that his parents had grounded him.

Sam sighed and opened his eyes. Part of him felt sorry that he'd tricked his parents and lied to Mrs. Goodman. But he knew that if he were given another chance he'd probably do it again. Performing had been magical in itself: the applause and the smiles. And he'd felt his uncle looking on from someplace close by.

"It was my fault," Charles had told him earlier as they sat on Sam's bed, feeling sorry for each other. "I thought it would be fun to visit you at your mother's office . . . to see what you were doing . . . and maybe help you."

Good old Charles. Sam smiled, remembering how sad Charles had looked—how sad and silly in his new haircut. Charles hardly ever admitted mistakes and Sam appreciated his admitting this one.

Sam's smile faded and he cleared his throat, even though he had nothing to say. Turning his head to the box on his left, he read a bumper sticker stretched across its side like a Band-Aid. "SKI IOWA," it said. Next to the bumper sticker was a crossed-out shipping address in New Zealand, the last place Uncle Frank had performed magic before he became too sick to travel. Before he died.

Sam felt in need of comfort. He also felt that he'd earned the right now to open at least one more of the boxes. He didn't think his mother would mind. He just didn't know which one to open. As he tried to decide, he found himself growing scared to open any of them. Even if he opened one every year—on his birthday, perhaps, or on Christmas Eve when he would normally have to wait until the next morning—eventually they would all be opened. And when that happened, there would be no more surprises from his uncle. It was a little like being told there would never again be another Christmas or another birthday. It was a little like being told he'd never eat chocolate again—only sadder.

Sam was tempted to shove the unopened boxes back under the bed.

"Knock, knock."

Sam turned to look at his bedroom door. His mother leaned against the doorframe, looking at him, her head tipped so that her ear almost rested on her shoulder.

"May I come in?" she asked in a voice that sounded as if she was afraid he might say no.

"Sure."

His mother stepped inside and walked around behind him. She brushed dust off the top of the SKI IOWA box and sat on it.

They were silent for several minutes, lost in their own thoughts. Sam looked at her, the dust dancing around her head, seeming to jump like fleas in and out of her hair. He almost smiled at this thought.

Then they both spoke at the same time.

"I . . ." Sam began.

"I just . . ." his mother began.

They looked at each other and Sam's mother chuckled. "I just wanted to tell you that before we took off for work on Friday, before you left the house and caught the bus for downtown, I noticed for the first time how much you look like Frank."

Sam recalled that morning and the uncomfortable stare his mother had given him before she left for work.

"It was his birthday, you know. On Friday."

Sam nodded. "I know." He studied his mother for signs of sadness. He saw sadness, especially in her eyes. "That's why I went to the park. It was a present . . . for Uncle Frank."

His mother nodded, her smile small and wilted. "And when we saw you in the park doing your magic, you looked so much like him when he was a boy. I just couldn't get over it. It made me feel like his kid sister again."

"I'm sorry I tricked you," Sam said, looking down at his feet. "I . . . I just didn't know what else to do." He peeked up at her.

She was smiling at him. "Oh, I don't know," she said. "If you had been honest and asked, we'd have said no. I've been thinking about it. I was angry with you when I found out. Some awful things could have happened to you. But then I wonder what *I* would have done if I were you." It was her turn to look at her feet. "I'd probably have done what you did."

She looked at the boxes and then at Sam. "Just don't do it again, O.K.? Ask us next time, will you? We'll work out something."

Sam nodded.

"Are you going to open up these boxes and see

what's inside? If you do, you'll just have to put everything back. We simply don't have room to spread out all of Frank's things."

Sam looked at the box his mother sat on. "I don't know if I should or not," he said quietly. "I'm . . . I'm afraid."

His mother sat up straighter. "Afraid of what?"

Sam was confused by his own feelings. He searched for words, the right words, but he couldn't find them. "I don't know." He struggled to make sense of his feelings. "I'm afraid that when I open these boxes, that will be it. No more Uncle Frank."

It hurt just to say those words—to admit out loud that his uncle was never coming back. He could see in his mother's face the same hurt that he felt.

"Well," his mother sighed, looking toward the ceiling. "*Frigate!*" She looked down at Sam and enjoyed the surprise on his face—surprise that she'd used his word. It had felt so good to say. "What do you think your Uncle Frank would want us to do?"

It had never occurred to Sam to ask that question. But as soon as his mother asked it, Sam knew the answer.

"He'd want us to open them up."

His mother's eyebrows shot up in surprise. "Us? Or just you?"

Again, the answer to her question was clear. "Us."

His mother frowned as she nodded, as if she wasn't sure if she agreed with Sam's answer to her question. After a few moments she stood and turned toward the box she'd been sitting on. "Should we start with this one?"

Sam began to roll up the sleeves of the jacket and then decided that opening boxes would be easier if he took it off. His mother took it from him and laid it on his bed.

Together they peeled the tape off the top of the box and lifted up the flaps. Sam leaned over the box to peer inside. He saw several smaller boxes wrapped in colorful paper, with ribbons tied around them. Lifting one out, Sam handed it to his mother, who unfolded a matching label taped to the box. She read aloud. "Open on Sam's birthday, 1991." She looked from the label to Sam. "That little joker." Her eyes smiled.

Sam reached for another box. He opened the label and read aloud. "Open on Frank's birthday, 1992."

One by one, Sam and his mother took packages out of the large box. Each label gave a year and an occasion on which Sam should open it—Christmas, Sam's birthday, Uncle Frank's birthday, Halloween.

"This isn't at all what I expected," Sam's mother said, as they repacked the box. "Let's open another big one." She sounded as excited as Sam felt.

Next to the SKI IOWA box was a short and wide one. Together they took off the tape and opened its flaps. Inside, on top, was a package wrapped in brown paper, paper that may have been cut from a grocery sack. In marker ink was printed, in wonderful curlicue letters: "OPEN NOW!"

His fingers trembling, Sam carefully peeled the tape off the ends of the package. He pulled back the paper slowly. Inside was a box of typing paper. Sam eased off the lid. On the very top was a sheet of paper addressed to Sam and his parents, covered with Uncle Frank's neat handwriting.

Dear Sam, Marjorie, and Seth,

By the time you read this, I'll be dead. It seems strange to write those words, but it's true. I wish I could be there when you open all of these packages, but I don't know where I'll be. I've got you covered until you're fifty, Sam, and by then you'll have lived longer than I have.

You're special, Sam. Just remember: Believing is seeing. Believe in magic and you'll see magic everywhere. Believe in love and love will surround you. Believe in beauty and you'll see beauty in the most surprising places. Believe in happiness and you'll see happiness even during the saddest times of life.

The rest of these pages are some stories that I wrote down for you to read whenever you like. Some of them are about my growing up and your mother will probably want to tell you I got a few things wrong. I probably did. Some of them are just stories I made up. Some of them made themselves up. And some of them aren't quite finished yet. But they're all about magic of one kind or another.

I hope you enjoy them.

Love,
Uncle Frank

Sam looked up from this note and saw tears in his mother's eyes. She blinked them away and sniffled. "Oh," she said, reaching into a pocket. "I almost forgot. I found this in the living room yesterday. I think it belongs to you. At least the

MARC TALBERT

has written a number of novels for middle readers and young adults in which he explores many issues of primary importance to young readers. His book *Toby* received a starred review in *School Library Journal* and was called "a work of rare power" by *Publishers Weekly*. Another book, *The Paper Knife*, which *Kirkus* noted "will hold readers while conveying a valuable message," was also the subject of a lengthy essay review in *Wilson Library Bulletin*.

Mr. Talbert and his wife live in Tesuque, New Mexico.

TOBY GOWING

is a young artist who has illustrated a number of children's books. *Double or Nothing* is her first book for Dial. Ms. Gowing and her husband live in Middletown, New Jersey.

date is correct." She held out a half-dollar coin and Sam took it from her, not believing what he was seeing.

He examined it closely. There was no mistaking it—this was the coin he'd lost. It had the nick on the nose of the coin's portrait of President Kennedy, from the time he dropped it on the sidewalk and stepped on it before he could stop himself.

Quicker than thinking, he flipped it up into the air. "Heads!" he cried as he caught it. But now that he'd flipped it, he was suddenly afraid to see if he'd guessed right.

He slapped it onto the back of his other hand and looked at his mother. "Would you look to see if . . ."

She nodded.

Sam looked up at the ceiling as he lifted his hand off the coin. Holding his breath, he waited for his mother to say . . .

"Heads."

Sam let out a sigh and looked down at the coin. *Believing is seeing.*

He slipped the coin into his pocket—the one without the hole. He felt it gradually warm up and melt into his leg. As if it were a part of him.

And it was.